Nina was quiet for a moment. Mateo wondered if she was lost in her own thoughts and hadn't heard him.

"Nina?" He noticed the frown on her face. Her hand trembled as she tucked a stray lock of hair behind her ear. Perhaps the adrenaline rush was wearing off and she was crashing, coming back to the reality of the situation. "Are you okay?"

"I... Yes, I'm fine. However, my vehicle is not." She pointed toward a cherry-red Trailblazer. One of the last left in the lot, other than his white Tahoe.

His heart kicked in his chest when he realized what had caused her distress.

"That vehicle there—" he gestured to it "—is yours?"

"Yes, the one with the slashed tires is mine." Her troubled gaze locked with his. "Detective Bianchi, do you know what this means?"

Yes, he sure did know.

"It means," he said slowly, "that if your attacker knows what car you drive, he clearly knows your identity."

And *that* put a whole new spin on things.

T0205144

Amity Steffen lives in northern Minnesota with her two boys and two spoiled cats. She's a voracious reader and a novice baker. She enjoys watching her sons play baseball in the summer and would rather stay indoors in the winter. She's worked in the education field for more years than she cares to count, but writing has always been her passion. Amity loves connecting with readers, so please visit her at Facebook.com/amitysteffenauthor.

Books by Amity Steffen

Love Inspired Suspense

Reunion on the Run
Colorado Ambush
Big Sky Secrets
Missing in Montana
Montana Hidden Deception

Visit the Author Profile page at LoveInspired.com.

Montana
Hidden Deception

AMITY STEFFEN

LOVE INSPIRED SUSPENSE
INSPIRATIONAL ROMANCE

LOVE INSPIRED® SUSPENSE
INSPIRATIONAL ROMANCE

ISBN-13: 978-1-335-98017-5

Montana Hidden Deception

Recycling programs
for this product may
not exist in your area.

Love Inspired
22 Adelaide St. West, 41st Floor
Toronto, Ontario M5H 4E3, Canada
www.LoveInspired.com

Printed in Lithuania

MIX
Paper | Supporting
responsible forestry
FSC® C021394

Behold, I will do a new thing; now it shall
spring forth; shall ye not know it? I will even make
a way in the wilderness, and rivers in the desert.
—*Isaiah* 43:19

For Ann Marie, whose strength, perseverance and vibrant personality shine through in everything you do. Your friendship, support and guidance over the decades have been a light in my world, especially through the darkest times.

ONE

Nina Montgomery began to carefully make her way down the steep incline. It was a perfect day to visit Mulberry Creek State Park. The rolling Montana sky seemed to stretch out forever from here. She'd departed from the trail to reach this higher elevation, hoping to get a few pictures of the newly hatched eaglets. What she had thought would be a good vantage point hadn't turned out to be that great. She'd gotten a few shots with the fancy Nikon camera her family had given her when she'd finished nursing school last year but doubted they were going to be anything spectacular.

It was no matter. The day was beautiful. The air was warm. The sun was shining. She'd just seen a momma raccoon with her kits trotting by. Nina loved springtime. Everything was fresh and new.

This is the day that the Lord has made, she thought. It was bright and glorious and perfect.

With measured footsteps, she edged her way downward. It would be mildly disastrous to take a tumble out here. If she twisted her ankle, it could take hours before someone else came this way. Nina already knew from past visits that cell phone reception could be spotty on this side of the park.

Almost to the trail now, she began to relax as the incline evened out. She held up her camera again. Last week, by chance, she'd taken a few good shots of a doe with her twin spotted fawns nestled in the woods. She stood still, using her zoom lens like a binocular.

She let out a gasp of surprise.

What was that? On the other side of the trail, movement.

Was it a bear? It was low to the ground, tucked in among the shrubbery. Rooting around.

No. It was too small to be a bear.

Her heart thumped harshly in her chest.

Was it a cub? That would not be good. Where baby was, momma was sure to be nearby. Her mind instantly whirled, trying to remember what to do if confronted by a bear. Make yourself as big as possible and try to appear frightening? Or curl into a ball and play dead? She couldn't recall.

Then the creature stood and she realized it wasn't a bear at all.

It was a man.

Odd.

He knelt down again, as if he'd only needed to stretch a moment.

Intrigued, Nina stood there watching him. Now that she was focused on him, she could see the man wasn't really rooting around at all. He wore thick black gloves along with his black sweats and his black hoodie. He had a garden trowel and he was digging a hole. What was he doing?

This was *really* odd.

Click.

Click.

Click. Click.

Almost reflexively, she snapped a few pictures.

Then she shook her head. What was she doing? It wasn't like her to spy on someone. He was probably just burying a time capsule. Or maybe he was geocaching. That had become popular lately.

Nina really had no idea what it entailed, other than leaving objects where other people could somehow find them. Did that include burying them?

Common sense told her she should keep moving. Just mind her own business. But her curiosity was burning hot and insatiable. She continued to move closer to the trail. For a moment, she contemplated simply asking what he was doing. But the man seemed to be working frantically now. Something about his movements, the way he viciously stabbed at the earth with the trowel, set her nerves on edge. Didn't people use their phones while geocaching? She wasn't sure, but that made her wonder if he was doing something else. But what?

Almost unconsciously, Nina slipped behind a tree. There was no way off this trail without strolling past the stranger. Suddenly, she did not want to do that. Instead, she lingered in her hiding place, feeling a bit foolish, but the old adage *better safe than sorry* swirled through her mind.

He stood again. This time he cast a glance over his shoulder. His features were mostly hidden under the hoodie he wore. Dark sunglasses covered much of his pale face. As she peered through thick branches, Nina thought it looked like he was scanning the area. She hoped the dense pine boughs would provide coverage for her.

He lifted a metal box that his body had been blocking. It wasn't much larger than a shoebox. For a moment, he just held it, almost reverently, then he lowered it into the hole.

At least he's not burying a body.

Nina pressed a hand to her chest, startled by the thought. Her heart pounded against her palm and she realized that this situation was making her more than a little uncomfortable.

The stranger grabbed the trowel again and with choppy, hurried movements, began filling the hole back in with the pile of dirt he'd accumulated. He tossed another glance over his shoulder. This time his gaze seemed to slowly scan the area. Could he sense her out there, watching?

Nina's heart was pounding so hard now she thought she could hear the blood sloshing through her veins.

Was she being ridiculous?

Maybe.

Better safe than sorry.

Moving slowly, she pulled her phone out of her pocket. No reception. Just as she'd expected. She stuffed it back inside. It was probably for the best. Who would she text and what would she tell them?

Don't worry about me. Watching a man dig a hole while I hide behind a tree.

Thinking of trees, she wished she'd found a bigger one to hide behind. She was grateful she'd thrown on dark jeans and a navy T-shirt this morning. It wasn't exactly camouflage, but at least it wasn't something that would stand out.

After what felt like forever, the man rose. She realized now he had a backpack. He shoved the thick black gloves and trowel inside. Then he scanned the area again. Thoroughly. Was he looking for someone? Something? Or was he just trying to commit the place to memory so he could come back later?

Dangling the backpack in his hand, he began to make his way out of the woods. He didn't have far to go. Maybe twenty feet or so. Nina saw that he held a can of spray paint.

First, he glanced up and down the trail, which caused her to look as well. There was no one in sight in either direction. Then, with his back to her, he shot a quick blast of black paint against the white bark of a birch. It was subtle, not something that would grab the attention of anyone hiking by. But it was obvious enough that someone looking for it would find it again.

The hole he'd dug was straight back from where he'd marked the spot. His hand tapped restlessly against his thigh. A minute later, he took a step into the tree line then stopped, as if debating what to do.

With a growl, he whirled and stomped out to the trail.

Nina realized she was holding her breath, pushing herself up against the tree as she tried to remain invisible and praying he would be on his way. She felt so alone, so secluded. It made her long to be at her family's ranch where there were kids and chaos. Really, she wished she was just about anywhere but here.

In another moment, he took off down the trail. Though his movements had seemed frantic, hurried, while he'd been digging, he seemed to be moving at a leisurely pace now. Or perhaps she was mistaken. Was his pace leisurely…or hesitant?

She watched him go and then her eyes swung across the path. From her position, she could just barely make out the black dirt covering the freshly dug hole.

Detective Mateo Bianchi was desperately trying to enjoy his day off. It was tough. Days off provided too much time to think. He'd hoped spending time at the Mulberry Creek State Park would refresh his mind, cleanse his spirit.

Leave him feeling invigorated.

Instead, it left him feeling drained. It wasn't due to jogging the trails, either. No. It was seeing all the families. Happy families with bickering kids, excited kids, exhausted kids.

Being here made him think of Josh and Nate. It made him miss them with that wretched ache that never went away. This was the sort of day where he and Jolene should've brought the twins to the park, had a picnic, enjoyed a hike.

But they were gone. Dead. His entire family. Killed in a horrific car crash two years ago. And he would probably never stop feeling as if he were to blame.

Maybe he didn't deserve to have a relaxing day.

Nate and Josh never would. Gone before their seventh birthday.

As his shoes smacked against the hard-packed earth, he glanced skyward, wondering for the millionth time why God had let it happen.

Knowing he wouldn't get an answer, he blew out a breath and tried to relax by taking in the view as he jogged along this out-of-the-way path. He scanned the brilliantly vibrant new spring foliage. It was admittedly beautiful against the flawless azure sky. He pulled in a lungful of fresh, clean air.

The trail curved and he glanced down in time to avoid a man rushing around the corner. Mateo stepped back and they barely missed smashing shoulders. They guy had his hood up, head down, and didn't even acknowledge Mateo.

Fine by him. He wasn't in the mood to chat with anyone, anyway. That's why he'd chosen this trail. It was on the edge of the park. There wasn't much to see, so it didn't get as much foot traffic as some of the others.

He glanced at his watch as he jogged along. It was nearing dinnertime and, as if it had just gotten the memo, his stomach growled. Maybe it was time to turn back. He wasn't a great cook but he was pretty good with the grill and he had a steak marinating in the fridge.

He slowed, ready to pivot, and nearly skidded in his tracks.

A woman stood inside the tree line, holding a metal box. Her long strawberry blonde hair was falling out of her ponytail. Dirt was smudged across her creamy-smooth cheek. Her pale green eyes were wide in surprise.

There was a pile of dirt at her feet.

Stranger still, she wore disposable gloves.

Her face scrunched, as if in embarrassment. "Detective Bianchi."

He arched a brow, surprised she remembered him from the one time they'd met. "Nina Montgomery, right?"

She gave him a hesitant smile and nodded. "I suppose you're wondering what I'm doing."

"Yes." He realized he was staring at her. She was such a strange, unexpected sight standing there in the trees, and he'd seen a lot of strange things over the years. "You could certainly say that."

She walked toward him, holding the box out in front of her like an offering. "It's an interesting story," she began.

"Can't wait to hear it."

"Hey!"

Mateo turned to see the man he'd nearly bumped into earlier racing toward them.

"Drop that box!"

His arm was outstretched and Mateo had seen enough weapons, even from a distance, to know the man was aiming a gun at them. He darted forward.

Nina let out a shriek, but instead of dropping the box as commanded, she dashed into the woods and took off running. Mateo tore after her, grateful she'd headed for the thickest foliage. He heard the unmistakable blast of a gun, muted by a silencer but audible all the same. Bark exploded on a tree off to their side.

Mateo grabbed Nina's hand as they ran. It made dodging foliage cumbersome, but it was better than being separated as the greenery became thicker and thicker. They dodged around trees, tore through bushes, and jumped over a few fallen logs.

The gunman was now shooting indiscriminately through the thick copse of trees. Bullets seemed to be flying on either side of them, taking out bark or sending up clumps of dirt as the slugs tore into the ground. His spine tingled—burned—with anxiety as he imagined a bullet tearing through his back.

Or Nina's.

God, protect us! The prayer took him by surprise. He hadn't prayed in years, but if he was going to start again, now seemed like as good of a time as any. The last time he'd prayed, he'd been begging for his child's life. It seemed God hadn't listened then.

Would he listen now?

What was in that box? How was Nina involved in this?

Though he barely knew the woman, his instincts told him she was not complicit in a crime. He knew both of her brothers and their wives. They were good people. Law-abiding people.

Was this a case of being in the wrong place at the wrong time?

What was it with her family? They were virtual trouble magnets. He had just helped her brothers through some pretty trying ordeals. Just last fall, her brother Seth had landed himself in the hospital after helping solve a child trafficking case. Nina had hovered over his bedside, scolding Mateo for questioning him while he was recovering from a concussion. She'd had spunk, but she hadn't deterred him.

Mateo risked a glance over his shoulder and saw nothing but trees.

"Who is that guy?" he asked.

"No idea." She tossed a quick look at him but kept moving. "It's a long story. I'll tell you all about it as soon as I can."

She would tell him later. That was for sure. Right now, he needed to concentrate on keeping them alive.

The park was enormous, covering thousands of acres. Would anyone hear the shooting? Would they question what it was, where it was coming from? Or would the sound be too muffled as it traveled over the dips and hills, through the trees and down the trails?

They ran and ran. The bullets had finally subsided. Either the man had run out of ammo or he had given up. Was he trying to track them, though? He looked over his shoulder, wondering if they'd left a trail through the trees. The greenery was fresh, new, and seemed to have sprung back into place. The ground was covered with last year's leaves. He didn't think they were leaving footprints anywhere.

"Here." He tugged Nina sideways then pulled her in beside him behind a massive boulder. It was one of many they had passed and wouldn't stand out any more than the others as an obvious hiding spot. "Get down."

She didn't hesitate, simply dropped down beside him. In the chaos, he hadn't realized she was still clutching the box. He saw it now, though, tucked under one arm.

Again, he wondered what it was holding that was so important.

She let out a soft groan.

"Are you hurt?" he asked, his voice low and concerned.

"Just apparently not in great shape," she whispered. "Stitch. In my side. Ouch. Or maybe I shouldn't be running after guzzling a bottle of water."

The Nikon camera dangling around her neck snagged his attention. "Any chance you got a picture of the guy?"

"Actually, yes."

Mateo felt hope spring up, but Nina immediately quashed it when she made an apologetic face.

Her voice was low as she spoke. "Unfortunately, he had his back to me the whole time. I honestly don't even know why I took the pictures. It was just a reflex. I'm sure I don't have anything useful."

"You never know. We'll have someone look at the pictures." *As soon as we get out of this*, he added silently.

He swiped sweat off his brow with the back of his hand. Then he scoured the forest, looking for any sign of the shooter. Had they lost the guy? He pulled his phone from his pocket. On a positive note, it was fully charged. Yet that didn't do a lot of good when they had no reception. Regardless, he sent off a few texts because he had to do *something*.

Nina shifted beside him. The box was now settled at her feet. She pulled off the disposable gloves that still baffled him and shoved them into the fanny pack she wore. When she glanced up at him, her expression was questioning.

Mateo gave her a warning look but didn't have to tell her not to speak.

She nodded to let him know she understood. Then she gave him a strained smile, as if to tell him she was okay. He patted her shoulder and then turned his attention to the woods. Mateo was grateful she was holding it together so well. He knew a lot of people would melt down under so much pressure. Being shot at? Chased through the woods? Targeted?

It was a lot to deal with. He'd been in law enforcement for more than a decade now and he still felt plenty rattled over what had just happened.

Yet there she sat, doing what sounded like deep breathing exercises. Or maybe she was simply trying to relieve the stitch in her side. He realized then that her eyes were closed and her hands were folded. In prayer? Probably.

They crouched there, hidden behind the boulder, both listening. They were so close their shoulders were touching. It was the only way to be sure they were both secreted. He glanced at his phone every few minutes, but none of the texts appeared to have been sent. Fifteen minutes passed. Then twenty. If he'd been alone, he may have begun creeping through the woods.

But he wasn't alone. He was with Nina and he was unarmed. A helpless sensation slithered through him. He hated feeling like he was cowering in the bushes, but for now he knew hiding was their best option.

He had so many questions for this woman.

Thirty minutes slipped by. He was torn because he didn't want to act hastily. He needed to be sure they weren't being stalked. Yet the longer they stayed hidden, the more time it gave the perp to get away.

Finally, he stood slowly and peered over the boulder.

His heart pounded as he waited for the sound of a gunshot.

TWO

Mateo had been glancing at his phone periodically. The scowl he wore let her know his text still hadn't gone through. Nina had contemplated sending a few texts of her own. But to what end? To whom? Her family? The last thing she wanted was to terrify them, to have them try to race to her rescue and potentially end up in danger themselves. No, she'd leave it to Mateo to report the situation.

When he stood, she found herself bracing for the worst. No shot came. In fact, there seemed to be no sign of the gunman at all. Mateo held out a hand and she reached for it. His strong fingers wrapped around her own and he hoisted her up. Her legs tingled from sitting crouched for so long.

"Do you think he's gone?" Her palms were sweaty and anxiety still buzzed down her spine.

"Not sure." Mateo turned to look at her. She hadn't remembered how dark his eyes were, almost as black as his hair. A worry line rested between his brows. He was taller than she remembered, too. She barely reached his shoulders. His gray thermal shirt stretched tautly across his chest. He looked formidable as he stood guard.

Nina was grateful that he was with her now. Detective Mateo Bianchi seemed to be the sort of man you would want on your side. What would she have done if the gunman had come back and she'd been alone? What if he'd sneaked up on her in the woods and Mateo hadn't been there?

She had a hunch he'd have shot her and she'd be dead right now. What had she stumbled upon? What could possibly be so important that someone would shoot at them? Had it only been a few hours ago that she'd been snapping photos of the eaglets? How had her day gone so completely sideways?

Nina wrapped her arms around herself, trying to keep it together.

"I think you need to tell me what's going on here." Mateo studied her face a moment before his gaze dropped to the box and then returned to her with a questioning look.

Nina told him everything, starting with how she'd been trying to get some photos of the eaglets. She described seeing the man in the woods and realizing he was burying something.

"Why didn't you just keep on walking?"

She winced. "I admit, I was curious at first. Then… I don't know. After I watched him for a minute, the situation started to feel off. People aren't supposed to litter. Burying something in the state park seemed odd to me. His behavior seemed strange and it made me think he wouldn't appreciate seeing me waltzing down the path. I started to get nervous, so I hid behind a tree until he left."

He arched a brow. "And then?"

"I was going to go back to my car, but my curiosity got the better of me." She could feel heat flood her cheeks at the admission. God had given her a great deal of common sense and most of the time she used it. She wasn't sure why today had been so different.

Then again, if she had gone to the parking lot, she would've run into the man on the trail when he'd backtracked. Would he have suspected her then? Would he have confronted her or just let her go? She would never know.

"You dug up the box."

She nodded though his tone implied that probably hadn't been a smart move. He was right, but she could hardly take it back.

"You just happened to have disposable gloves to wear to keep your hands clean?" His pitch was skeptical.

Nina knew it was a legitimate question and even understood his incredulity. She patted the fanny pack her brothers liked to tease her about. "I'm a nurse, if you recall."

"I do."

"I keep a few emergency items in here. Gauze, scissors, tape, some antiseptic wipes." She unzipped the pack to give him a view of what was inside. "A few pairs of disposable gloves. I worked in the ER long enough to realize accidents happen all the time. I like to be prepared. I've never had to use my supplies for anything worse than a kiddo with a skinned knee, but you never know."

"I see." He knelt down in front of the box then gave the latch a tug. "It's locked."

"Yes." She shrugged. "When I realized I couldn't open it, I was going to put it back where I found it. I thought about letting a park ranger know on my way out today, but then you came along."

"Then we were shot at." He pinched the bridge of his nose. "Why didn't you drop the box when he told you to?"

Why hadn't she?

"I barely remember him saying that. All I remember is that I heard him yell. I saw a gun and my instinct was to run."

"It was a pretty good instinct. The trees are so thick out

here, he wasn't able to get off a clear shot. Running into the woods likely saved our lives. I wonder why he came back."

She thought about that a moment. "After he marked the tree, he seemed hesitant to leave. At one point, he even went back into the woods."

"Did you ever get a good look at him?"

"No. He had his hood up the whole time and sunglasses on. Even when he was in the woods."

"I ran into him on the trail." Mateo's gaze flittered around, still taking in their surroundings. "I didn't get a good look at him, either. He had his head down and his face was covered. Seemed like he was in a hurry to get out of the park."

"He must've changed his mind."

"Obviously, whatever is in that box is pretty important to him. I'm going to bring it to the station and find out what's inside." He eyed the fanny pack that she'd zipped shut. "Did I see a plastic bag in there? I know you've touched the box, and I doubt we can lift any prints off it after it was buried in the dirt, but it might not hurt to try."

Nina pulled the plastic grocery bag out and handed it to him. "I keep a few in there in case I come across litter."

His lips twitched. "Right. I gather you're not a fan of littering."

"No." She watched as he bagged the box. Then he checked his phone. She could tell by his expression that he had no news. She felt jittery and wanted nothing more than to leave the park. "Can we get out of here now?"

"Maybe."

Mateo was hyperaware of his surroundings as his eyes scanned the forest. Birds chirped above him and a chipmunk stared him down, scolding him for invading the pristine space. Other than that, he and Nina seemed to be alone out here. He saw no questionable movement, heard no troubling sounds of someone approaching.

Still, he hated being weaponless. With Nina beside him, he wasn't about to take any chances.

He glanced at her. Her cheeks were rosy and her green eyes seemed to glint in the sunlight. She looked young—so innocent and delicate—though he knew she was old enough to have graduated from nursing school.

She had also mentioned she worked in the ER, so maybe she wasn't as delicate as she appeared. He had to assume that took nerves of steel some days. That probably explained how she'd taken being shot at so well.

He cleared his throat when he realized he'd been gazing into her lovely eyes a few seconds too long. What was wrong with him?

"Uh, yeah." He kept his tone low, just in case. "I think we're in the clear."

"Good," she said decisively, "because I do not enjoy being shot at. That is not a good way to spend the day."

It took him a moment to realize she was trying to bring some levity to the serious situation.

His lip quirked. "Being shot at is not one of my favorite things, either."

"I suppose you've had more practice at it than I have." She shrugged. "Considering that this is my first, and hopefully last, time."

Surprised by her humor, he nodded his agreement. "I have been shot at a time or two, so I agree. I could do without that particular sort of excitement."

"You didn't shoot back." Her eyes scanned over him as if searching for a hidden weapon. "I suppose that's because you're off duty." Her tone held curiosity rather than censure. "At least, I assume you are since you're at the state park and you were out for a jog."

It was a stark contrast to Jolene's reproachful voice that, even now, years later, slammed through his brain.

Honestly, Mateo, do you even know how to enjoy a day off? Who carries a gun to the county fair? For once, can you act like you aren't on duty?

He rubbed his fingers over his forehead, as if he could scrub her words away. The last few years with her had been rough. She had complained about his job nonstop, had made him feel as if it was nothing but an inconvenience to her. He had tried to explain that, with all the ugly things he'd seen, he appreciated the added protection of a weapon.

Even on his day off.

So today, out of respect for her, he had eyed the gun locker that held his sidearm and had decided to leave it behind. He didn't want to think of Jolene right now. He needed to push her out of his mind so he could concentrate on the current situation.

"I'm not armed," he admitted.

Her gaze darted around the forest as if fearing their pursuer was lurking just out of sight.

"We're going to head back, but I don't want to go the same way we got here." He didn't have to voice his concern that the man could be waiting for them, either on the trail, or lingering a ways off. "We'll cut through the woods but head toward the fire tower."

The structure stood near the entrance of the park. It was the biggest tourist attraction in the place. Once they were out of the thickest part of the trees, it should be visible and they could use it to guide them to the ranger station.

She frowned and patted her pack. "A compass is one thing I don't have with me."

He tugged the long sleeve of his thermal shirt up an inch, allowing her to see his wrist. "Fortunately, this good old-fashioned watch has a built-in compass."

The watch had been a gift from the twins, given to him on the last Christmas they'd had together. Sure, Jolene had paid for it. But Nate and Josh had proudly told him it had been their idea and they had picked it out. They'd thought it would be useful for the family camping trip planned for the following summer.

It was a trip they'd never gotten to take.

He tucked the memory away and studied the compass for a moment. Then he nodded toward the east. "Heading this way should lead us to the fire tower. We'll stay in the woods but walk parallel to the trail. Sound good?"

"Getting out of here sounds great."

He picked up the bag holding the box. The sooner they got out of here, the sooner he could find out what was inside.

They were quiet for a while as they pushed through brush and brambles. Mateo checked the compass periodically to be sure they were still on track.

"Thank God you came along when you did," Nina said, finally breaking the silence.

He frowned. "We were shot at and you're thanking God?"

"For the fact that you came along? *Yes*." She gave him a quizzical look. "Don't tell me you don't believe in God."

"I do believe." He inwardly grimaced over the fact that a conversation with a woman he barely knew had headed in this direction. He believed, all right. He wouldn't be so angry with God right now if he *didn't* believe. No way was he getting into all of that.

Then again, he reminded himself, he had prayed today. More than once.

God had heard his prayer, answered it, because they were both alive and safe.

His phone chimed and Nina looked at him in surprise.

Mateo was surprised as well.

He tugged it from his pocket.

It was a text from Officer Lainie Hughes, one of the three people at the department he'd sent a message to, hoping that at least one would go through. He had known she was on duty today, so she'd been sent the first message.

"You have service?" Nina asked.

"Barely," he admitted. "But one of my texts went through to one of the officers in the department. She said the park rangers were alerted and that back up is en route." He glanced at his watch. "But the shooter could be long gone. The last shot fired was edging on an hour ago. That would be more than enough time for him to have jogged back down the trail and gotten out of the park."

He tried placing a call to Officer Hughes.

It didn't go through, so he typed another text instead, then watched in frustration as the screen indicated it had been sent but not delivered. He shoved the phone back in his pocket, grateful that help was on the way.

While behind the boulder, he'd indicated to Officer Hughes that shots had been fired. Now, he had to assume that the park's entrances were being blocked off by rangers and that the park was being systematically evacuated. It was too bad that the shooter, if he had any sense, had probably hightailed it out of there already. It was unfortunate the text had taken so long to go through.

"Do you hear that?" Nina asked.

He froze. "What?"

Had she heard someone stalking them? He'd been so lost in his own thoughts, he realized he hadn't been paying attention. A stupid and potentially dangerous move.

Then he heard it.

"Sirens," she said.

Yes, sirens. Help was on the way.

That realization seemed to give Nina renewed energy as she quickened her pace.

"Let's veer this way," he suggested after glancing at the compass again. "We should hit the trail sooner rather than later. We're far enough away from where we entered that it's unlikely the perp would be lingering. Besides, if he hasn't vacated the park already, I suspect the approaching sirens will have him on the run."

In a matter of minutes, they were back on the trail, near the incline they had tumbled over. The fire tower loomed in the distance. Though Mateo didn't believe the shooter was still hanging around, he remained vigilant just in case. Desperate criminals were known to be unpredictable and he had to believe the man was desperate to retrieve the metal box.

Nina's phone erupted in a cacophony of sounds, a myriad of alerts as text messages from various people finally came through. She pulled her phone out and scrolled as they hustled along.

"My family just heard about an active shooter in the park. They're checking in to see if I'm okay." She began tapping out replies. "I'm going to let them know I'm fine. I'm not going to tell them I was the target. At least, not right now. If I did that, the whole family would think they need to race to my rescue."

Mateo smirked at that.

"Good call. I met your family when I was helping your

brothers out. I think you're right. They'd be here in a heart-beat. Since I'm sure the park is being cleared out, the last thing we need is more people showing up." He tilted his head to the side, listening as the hum of a motor caught his attention.

"That sounds like a side-by-side," Nina said. "We have one at the ranch."

The sound got louder, indicating the vehicle was headed their way. It rounded a bend and Nina was right, it was a side-by-side.

Officer Lainie Hughes was behind the wheel. She waved when she spotted them. A moment later, she reached them.

"Am I ever glad to see you," Mateo proclaimed.

"Likewise." Lainie eyed them up. "You're both okay?"

"Fortunately," Mateo said.

"I commandeered this from one of the park rangers. Hop on." She patted the empty seat beside her. "I'll fill you in on the way back to the parking lot."

Nina slid in first then Mateo. With three of them on the bench seat, it was a tight fit, but he wasn't about to complain.

"The rangers have been emptying out the park, checking everyone as they leave, taking down license plate numbers. You know the drill. So far, no one has admitted to seeing anything. A handful of parkgoers claimed they thought they heard a few rounds shot off, but they assumed it was firecrackers."

"He was using a silencer," Mateo said.

"I expected as much," Lainie admitted.

They reached the parking lot, which was mostly cleared out of cars, except for several cruisers. It was swarming with law enforcement and park rangers. Mateo presumed the other three lots, located in different areas of the park, would look about the same.

"I should have asked…" Lainie said to Nina. "What lot are you parked in?"

Mateo hadn't thought to ask, either, believing she was parked here as it was closest to where she'd been hiking. Yet he should have confirmed.

Nina was quiet for a moment. Mateo wondered if she was lost in her own thoughts and hadn't heard Officer Hughes.

"Nina?" He noticed the frown on her face. Her hand trembled as she tucked a stray lock of hair behind her ear. Perhaps the adrenaline rush was wearing off and she was crashing, coming back to the reality of the situation. "Are you okay?"

"I…yes, I'm fine. However, my vehicle is not." She pointed to a cherry-red Trailblazer. One of the last left in the lot, other than his white Tahoe.

His heart kicked in his chest when he realized what had caused her distress.

"That vehicle there—" he gestured to it "—is yours?"

"Yes, the one with the slashed tires is mine." Her troubled eyes locked with his. "Detective Bianchi, do you know what this means?"

Yes, he sure did know.

"It means," he said slowly, "that if your attacker knows what car you drive, he clearly knows your identity."

And *that* put a whole new spin on things.

THREE

Nina couldn't take her eyes off her Trailblazer. Mateo circled the vehicle and she followed. All four tires had been slashed. She shuddered. Not just because of the damage, but because of the realization that her attacker had apparently been armed with a knife as well as a gun. Worst of all, clearly, he knew her. What did the slashed tires mean? Was it just supposed to slow her down? Was it a warning? A threat? It felt like a threat. If he knew what SUV she drove, what else did he know about her?

What if God hadn't sent Mateo to her when He had? What if the man had overpowered her and dragged her off the trail and into the woods?

She could *not* let her mind go there.

"Nina?" Mateo sidled up next to her. His hand floated in the air a moment, as if he wanted to reach out and give her assurance, but then it fell to his side. "Are you okay?"

She had never been good at lying. Now didn't seem the best time to start.

"Actually," she said, "I don't think I am."

"I can talk to Officer Hughes. She can take you home. Better yet, she can take you to your family's ranch. I suspect you'll be safer there."

Nina pulled her gaze away from the shredded tires.

"I want to go to the station with you." Her eyes locked with his. "I want to see what's in that box."

His brow furrowed and he was clearly ready to protest. Nina did not give him the chance.

"Please, Detective. I've been chased, shot at, and my tires are slashed. Don't you think I deserve to know what's so important to this guy?"

"I guess it wouldn't hurt to have you come along to the department. I can take your official statement." He shrugged. "Who knows, maybe something in that lockbox will help you figure out who this guy is. I mean, he clearly knows who you are, which leads me to believe that even if you didn't recognize him, you likely know him as well."

She nodded slowly. "I thought of that. I've been wracking my brain, trying to place him. It's hard when I don't even know where to start. I grew up in Mulberry Creek. It could be someone I went to school with. Someone I worked with in the past, or present, or volunteer with."

"Could be someone from your church."

She frowned at him.

"I'm not ruling anyone out," he said.

"Are you always so cynical?"

"Yes." He motioned toward the only other civilian vehicle in the lot. "Let's go. The crew here is capable of handling things. Officer Hughes is currently viewing the security footage of the parking lot. She'll meet us back at the station."

He opened the door of the white SUV for Nina. She hopped inside.

"I'd like to check in with the officers on scene, if you don't mind," Mateo said. "Will you be okay if I do that? I won't go far and I won't be long. You'll be safe."

"Of course." She nodded for emphasis. "Take your time."

He gently closed her door.

She watched as he strode over to a group of uniformed men and women. He looked so confident, strong and capable. He shoved his hands into his pockets as he spoke with the group, as if he was completely relaxed after the whole ordeal.

Nina settled into the seat and realized his vehicle smelled like him. Like woodsy soap and faint cologne. It was comforting. In fact, everything about Mateo was comforting.

She realized she also found his dark good looks and his deep, smooth voice appealing. In fact, she found everything about the man quite likeable.

You were just shot at, she thought, *and now you're thinking of Mateo's espresso-colored eyes.*

"I do love espresso, though," she murmured to herself.

As she waited for him, her gaze scanned the lot, the woods on the edge, even drifted to the tower behind them. She had been coming to this park for as long as she could remember. How many picnics, hikes and leisurely days had she spent here with her family?

Would she ever feel safe coming here again?

The memory of being shot at, the intense fear she had felt, slammed into her. It had been a terror unlike anything she had ever known.

She closed her eyes and leaned her head back.

"Breathe," she muttered under her breath. "Just breathe."

She was exhaling slowly when Mateo opened the driver's-side door and climbed in. She glanced at him. He quirked a brow at her but didn't say anything, just started up his Tahoe and slowly drove from the lot.

"Is there *anything* about the man that seemed familiar?" Mateo asked once they were out of the park. "His stance? His tone?"

Nina desperately tried to recall something, anything, that would be helpful. She came up blank.

"No," she said, feeling as if she were letting Mateo down. He must've heard the defeat in her voice.

"It's all right," he said soothingly. "It's been an afternoon. You have a lot to process. I'm sure your mind is spinning."

It *was* spinning and she was grateful that he recognized that.

"If anything comes to you later—"

"I'll be sure to let you know."

"I've got to be honest… I'm concerned about your safety. When is your next shift at the hospital?"

"The hospital?" Nina echoed. Then she recalled she had mentioned she had been an ER nurse. "Oh, I don't work in the ER anymore. I'm a hospice nurse now. Have been for the past three months."

"Really?" Mateo's tone implied he wasn't sure what to make of that. "That sounds…heavy."

"It can be, yes," Nina said. "I'm supposed to work the day after tomorrow."

"Any chance you can have someone cover for you?"

Nina frowned. She hated the idea of shirking her responsibilities. Though, it was a new client, one she hadn't met, which made allowing someone to replace her a bit less difficult.

"Nina, your life could be on the line here." Mateo's tone was soft but his words hit hard.

"I know," she murmured. "Yes, I'm sure if I explain the situation, my supervisor can replace me for a day or two."

"You may need to be out more than a day or two."

"I can't even think about that right now."

Her phone rang and she tugged it from her pocket. It was her mother. She silenced the call and instead sent a text simply stating she couldn't talk at the moment, that she was fine, and would check in soon.

Then she powered off the device.

"Not ready to talk to anyone yet?" he asked.

"It's my mom. If I answer, she'll sense how wrong everything is, force the truth out of me, and then panic until she sees for herself that I'm okay. It's best if I can just cut to the part where she can see that I'm okay. I'll tell my family what happened, I sure won't be able to keep it a secret, but it's best if I do it in person."

"Good plan. Your family is pretty great. They'll be sure to keep you safe."

"Do you have family?" Nina voiced the question without thinking. Mostly, she was trying to make conversation, trying to distract herself from what had happened in the park. Mateo's frown and hesitation made her wish she could take the question back. Before she had a chance to try, he spoke.

"Of course. I mean…yeah, I have parents, you know." He cleared his throat. "They're retired and spend a good deal of their time traveling the country in their RV. I also have a sister. Mara. She lives in Bozeman. She's a kindergarten teacher."

"That's nice."

That's nice? She mentally chastised herself, embarrassed that she couldn't think of anything else to say. Maybe it was best to say nothing because his hesitant tone implied it was something he did not want to talk about.

They finished the short drive to Mulberry Creek in silence.

Once at the police department, he escorted her inside to his office where she—again—went over the details of what she had seen. This time he took notes and his questions seemed even more thorough than before. Nina wished desperately that she had better answers for him. Yet, try as she might, she could not make out anything familiar about her attacker.

A knock on the door grabbed their attention.

"Come in," Mateo called.

The door was already open a crack. Officer Joe Rollins, whom Nina vaguely knew because he was close in age to her brothers, came in.

"I'm just letting you know we managed to get the box open. You said you wanted to go through the contents yourself. It's ready whenever you are."

"Great!" Nina stood up so fast her chair squealed as it slid backward.

Mateo glared at her.

She shot him a look right back. "Please don't make me beg. You said yourself, since this guy knows me and I probably know him, the contents might give me a clue as to who he is."

Nina had no idea if the evidence would rattle anything loose in her brain, but she had to try. She wanted this man caught. The thought of him lurking out there, strolling the streets of Mulberry Creek, possibly bringing harm to others, did not sit well with her.

"Fine." Mateo stood. "You can stay to the back of the evidence room."

"Perfect." She grinned at him. "I promise I'll stay out of the way. You'll hardly know I'm there."

You'll hardly know I'm there.

Nina's words seemed to taunt Mateo. He knew she was there all right. He was far too aware of her presence. It had been impossible to ignore her excitement as he'd led her to the evidence room. He was also very aware of how that exuberance faded with each item he pulled out of the box.

So far, Officer Rollins had helped him log nearly a dozen items, primarily jewelry. They'd taken pictures, jotted notes into the log book, and inspected the items from every angle, looking for initials, engravings, or any type of clue.

Nina sighed.

Mateo glanced up at her.

"Sorry," she muttered, "it's just that the box is almost empty and nothing is familiar."

He shrugged as he gingerly held a Rolex in his gloved hand. Officer Rollins had done a quick internet search and deemed the Rolex was high-end and worth a small fortune. "It was a long shot. We both knew that."

Officer Rollins finished logging the watch then bagged it up.

Next, Mateo pulled a zippered sandwich bag out of the lockbox.

Officer Rollins let out a low whistle. "Those are all American Gold Eagle coins. My grandad is big into coins. Has quite the collection. I'm not nearly the expert he is, but I'd say you're looking at well over ten grand in that bag."

"This guy's bounty is definitely adding up," Mateo agreed. His rough calculation had the contents at close to a hundred grand.

Once the coins were processed, Mateo pulled out another piece of jewelry.

Nina pushed away from the wall where she'd been leaning, though she was careful not to get too close.

"That's stunning," she said.

Mateo held up the diamond-studded crucifix so she could get a better look. It was a large pendant hanging from a gold chain.

"Truly beautiful." Her brow furrowed. "I…"

He waited. When she said nothing, he gave her a verbal nudge. "You what? Have you seen this before?"

"I don't think so." She shook her head, looking uncertain. "Maybe? I'm not sure. It grabbed my attention, but that could be because it's so striking."

He motioned her forward and she came in for a better look. It laid flat against his gloved palm.

She bit her lip as her eyes scanned over it. Finally, she glanced at him. "I just don't know. I want so badly to be helpful. Now I'm not sure if it's truly familiar to me or if I just want it to be."

She looked so utterly disappointed.

"Don't worry about it," Mateo urged. "There are a few more items left. Let's get them logged and then wrap this up."

He pulled out a few more antiques that he suspected would be worth a fair amount.

Last, he retrieved a large ruby brooch. No one had to tell him it was quite valuable. The size alone made that clear.

"What happens now?" Nina asked.

"We'll run the items through the system," Officer Rollins chimed in. "It's likely they are stolen. It's such an eclectic mix. Hopefully, at least a few of them will turn into leads."

"We'll also get an expert for appraisals," Mateo added. "I'm curious about the overall value. Also, bringing in someone from the field may help us figure out where some of these items originated." He spent a few minutes finishing up with the evidence, then peeled off his gloves and led Nina from the room.

Officer Hughes caught them in the hallway.

"Sir!" she called.

He pivoted.

"You asked for an update on the incident in the parking lot," she said. "The security cameras picked up a man slashing Miss Montgomery's tires. He was, as you described, the attacker. Dark clothes, hoodie pulled up. There isn't a clear shot of his face. He was quick about it, then darted away out of camera range. He wasn't picked up anywhere else in the park. I suspect he had a change of clothes in that backpack. Or, all he'd really have to do is peel off the hoodie and his look would change. Regardless, though we don't have anything useful yet, we'll go over footage from the other parking lots for the entire day."

Mateo nodded. "I appreciate the update."

Officer Hughes hurried off, likely to deal with the next crisis.

Mateo turned to Nina. "Are you ready to go home?"

She wrapped her arms around herself and nodded. Her hair had been put neatly back into a ponytail and, after a trip to the restroom, the smudge on her cheek had been cleaned off. Still, she looked rattled and he wished he could do something to make her feel better. He knew she probably just needed time to process and work through everything.

"By home, I mean your family's ranch," he clarified. "Are you okay with that? I can take you there now."

"Would it be too much to ask to stop by my house first?" She gave him an apologetic yet hopeful look. "I'd like to pick up some clothes. I could have my parents or one of my brothers take me. However, once they find out what happened, I know things are going to get chaotic. They'll have a million questions and go into protective mode. They'll probably want to put me in a bubble and lock me away. I know you're busy. If you don't have time, I completely understand. I'd go myself, if I had a vehicle."

"It's not a problem," he said. "In fact, I'd rather take you. Once you get situated at the ranch, I plan on having a police presence there. I'd prefer once that's in a place that you didn't leave."

"A police presence." She blew out a breath. "I can't believe this morning I was excited about eaglets. Now I need police protection."

"I'm also going to take a cruiser instead of my personal vehicle. If this guy is watching us, I want it to be clear you are under police protection. I'm hoping that'll be a deterrent."

Once he'd checked out the vehicle he needed, they headed toward the door.

"Detective Bianchi, I want you to know I appreciate everything you did for me today. I know you're going to catch this guy," she said.

He had worked hard to earn the title of detective and usually he enjoyed hearing it. Not now, though. It sounded too formal coming from Nina's lips.

"Call me Mateo," he said gruffly. "After running for our lives together, 'Detective Bianchi' sounds a bit too formal."

She smiled at him. It was her first true smile of the day, lighting up her eyes and setting a dimple in her left cheek free. His heart seemed to swirl in his chest. Perhaps he should have kept the formality in place.

Too late now.

"Where are we headed?" Mateo asked.

Nina rattled off the address.

"I feel like I know that place but I'm not sure why."

"I bought the house from my sister-in-law, Holly," Nina admitted. "I know you were there last year, working on her case."

"That's right." He used his key fob to unlock a cruiser

with the department's logo on the side and then opened Nina's door for her. She thanked him as she got in.

He was intent on keeping the conversation light as he drove toward her home. Thinking the best way to do that was to ask for updates on her brothers, he did just that. All the while, he remained vigilant, needing to be sure they were not being followed.

"Eric and Cassie recently had twins."

His heart pinched though he knew that they had been expecting twins. He couldn't help but think of his own boys.

"Ethan and Matilda," Nina continued. "Named after Cassie's grandparents. Wyatt is really excited about being a big brother. Seth and Holly are expecting a baby boy in about a month. Chloe is not nearly as excited about being a big sister. I'm pretty sure she'll change her mind once the baby is here."

He continued to pepper her with questions that had nothing to do with the attacker. She seemed to relax and was all too happy to talk about her new nieces and nephews.

In no time, he was turning off the blacktop and onto a gravel road.

"Second mailbox on the left?" He was pretty sure that was correct. He'd been here a few times last year when Holly and her daughter Chloe had been attacked.

"Good memory," she said.

"How long have you had the place?"

"Almost half a year. I had been renting, but when Holly married my brother and mentioned she was selling her house, it seemed like it was meant to be."

"Cute place."

Mateo eyed the pale blue house with white trim and shutters. A white front porch held flowerpots filled with magenta hydrangeas.

"Thanks." Nina beamed at him. "I kind of love it. I grew up with a house full of siblings then had four roommates in nursing school. It's really nice to have a place of my own."

He maneuvered the vehicle so it was facing the road. He was sure they hadn't been followed, but he was anxious to be on their way again.

Nina hopped out and he hustled after her.

"I'll be quick." She had already pulled out her key and quickly slid it in the lock. "I'll just throw stuff into my biggest suitcase. If I forget anything, someone at the ranch is sure to have something I can borrow."

They stepped into the entryway. A suspicious scent assaulted Mateo's senses. He realized, almost subconsciously, that they were about to die.

"No!" He shouted the word as Nina reached for the light switch. In one swift movement, he latched onto her arm, tugged her back out the door and shoved her across the lawn, propelling her forward. "Run!"

Even as they raced across the grass, the unmistakable scent of natural gas still lingered in his nose. They were halfway to the tree line when—

Boom!

The blast blew him forward, slammed him into Nina. He instinctively wrapped his arms around her, protecting her body with his. They hit the ground as the world around them exploded.

FOUR

Nina slammed against the hard-packed earth, her mind swirling in confusion as pain from the jarring tumble ricocheted through her body.

"You okay?" Mateo asked, his voice gruff. He shifted and it was only then that she realized he'd landed on top of her. He'd shielded her, if the blood trickling down his temple was any indication.

"I'm fine." Her response was breathless and her voice wobbled. "But you're hurt."

"Nope, I'm good." He scrambled off her then held out a hand, but she was already clambering to her feet.

"My *house*!" Her words held equal parts disbelief and horror as she caught sight of the inferno blazing behind them. She swayed and Mateo reached out to steady her.

With his hand firmly against her back, he said, "We need to get out of here. This was a natural gas explosion. You didn't flip the light switch or do anything to spark it. I think it was set remotely. I have no idea how far away the guy is."

He didn't need to spell it out for her. Nina understood he thought the attacker may be nearby. The very thought made her blood run cold.

They were instantly on the move, jogging on shaky legs to the cruiser.

"Close enough to know we went inside?" Nina guessed.

Mateo didn't answer.

He didn't need to.

Nina could sense his tension and it only added to her own. She tossed a worried glance over her shoulder and wouldn't have been surprised to see the man lingering in the tree line. Or racing after them, gun raised.

All she saw was her house, her home, blazing. Already, ash and smoke permeated the air, mixing with the debris from the blast.

Mateo ushered her into the cruiser. She tumbled inside, frantically looking around at the disaster. How could everything have changed so quickly? It was almost incomprehensible. Only moments ago, she'd been looking at the home she'd been so proud of purchasing on her own.

She was vaguely aware of Mateo calling in the incident. Her mind seemed to fluctuate between disbelief and horror. She was in shock, she knew, and needed to shake herself out of it.

"The fire department is on the way." Mateo's tone was terse as the cruiser tore out of the driveway. "Officer Rollins is only a few minutes out. He'll get here quickly to keep an eye on the fire until the trucks arrive. I hate leaving the scene, but if this guy is still hanging around here, I don't want to give him the chance to take another shot at us."

She knew he meant literally and the somber realization pulled her from her stupor.

"I don't get it." Nina pulled in a breath, blew it out again, trying to calm herself as trees whizzed by in a blur. She realized he had turned north, headed toward the ranch, rather than south, which would lead back to town and the direction the emergency vehicles would be coming from. "What in that box could be so important? Sure, some of the items may be worth a lot of money, especially when added all together. But enough money to *kill* for?"

She just couldn't grasp the lunacy of that.

She turned to face him, studying him.

Mateo's expression was grim. His eyes swung from the road in front of them to the rearview mirror as he kept watch from all directions.

"Yeah." He glanced at her, their eyes locking only briefly before he returned his attention to the road. "This all seems a bit excessive. Too excessive. My gut instinct, and a decade of experience, are telling me that there's way more to this than some potentially stolen items."

Reality slammed back into Nina then full-force. She realized Mateo was still bleeding from the wound that he'd received during the blast. His dark hair seemed to be matted with blood, but he'd apparently swiped away the trickle that had slid down his cheek.

"You're hurt." Her heart lurched. She shifted in her seat and fumbled to unzip the fanny pack her brothers always made fun of. She pulled out a large gauze pad and tore open the package. "Let me help with that."

He shot her a sideways look. "It's fine."

"It's not." She gently pressed the gauze pad to his temple. "You blocked me from the flying debris. Are you hurt anywhere else?"

"No."

"You're lying," Nina accused. She pulled a butterfly bandage from her supply.

He shot her a look.

She shot him one right back. "What I meant to say is, thank you for protecting me. Did you get hit anywhere else?" She deftly attached the bandage over his wound.

He hesitated and it was clear he didn't want to admit to anything.

"Mateo, either you give an honest answer or I'm going to assume the worst."

"Fine. Something hit me in the back. Clipped my shoulder." He scowled. "It clobbered me, but don't think it cut me. Doesn't feel like it's bleeding. Just sore."

Sore.

Nina assumed it was much more than sore. She was certain he'd been pummeled by debris, yet he refused to utter a word of complaint. Her admiration for this man seemed to grow by the minute.

"We're just about to the ranch." He pointed out the obvious in a clear attempt to distract her. "How are you doing? Ready to face your parents?"

Nina let out a mirthless laugh. "Not even a little. I wish I didn't have to tell them. But—"

"The rumor mill in Mulberry Creek is running strong. They'd find out anyway."

"Right." She leaned back in her seat and sighed. "The story better come from me. And you. You'll stay to help fill in the details, right? You're not going to just drop me off in the driveway?"

He slid her a look. "I'm not going anywhere for a while. Not until I get an update on your house."

Her house.

She couldn't let herself think of that right now. It was only a house. It was replaceable.

Almost as an afterthought, she flipped down the sun visor and was relieved to find there was a built-in mirror on the backside. She gasped when she flipped it open. She had something—soot, perhaps—smudged across her face. There was debris in her hair. Grass, twigs…splinters?

She groaned. "You could have warned me that I'm a disaster."

He quirked a brow. "My mother would not approve of me telling a woman she's a disaster."

"Now is not the time for chivalry." She managed to find a wet wipe and began to clean up her face. "I'm not being vain." She finished with her face and started to pluck at her tresses, all the while wishing she had a comb in her fanny pack, but alas she did not. "It's just that my parents *cannot* see me like this."

"It's nice of you to care so much."

She shot him a look, wondering for just a moment if he was mocking her.

"Your family seems really close."

"We are." She continued to try to tidy her hair. "You probably know my older sister, Ella, died several years ago. The first few years were tough, but I think in the end, it brought us closer together. I'm the youngest of the family. Whether I like it or not, my parents will always think of me as their baby girl."

"Is that a bad thing?" His brow furrowed, as if he were genuinely curious.

"It can be overwhelming sometimes. Yet I know it's only because they love me. So, no, it's not a bad thing." She gave herself another once-over. Satisfied that she'd cleaned up as best she could, Nina flipped the mirror closed and readjusted the visor again.

Mateo flipped on the blinker, indicating he was about to turn into the driveway and pass under the wrought-iron arch that announced Big Sky Ranch in chunky iron letters. The winding driveway split in two. Mateo took the branch to the right, which would lead to her parents' home, and

Eric's, if he were to keep driving. Seth's house was in the other direction.

Nina felt a wave of comfort when she spotted the log structure. It had just been rebuilt—due to a fire, ironically.

It wasn't the place she had grown up in. Eric and his family had taken that over and lived just up the hill. Even so, she'd spent plenty of hours in this new house. It didn't matter that the building was new, home was where the heart was. And there was plenty of heart in this log abode to go around.

Mateo hadn't even parked the cruiser when her parents, James and Julia, rushed out onto the porch.

"Looks like they've been watching for you."

Nina's heart pinched. Her family had been through so much this year. She knew how worried her parents must be. She realized belatedly that she should have at least mentioned that Mateo was bringing her home. It was probably a shock to see a cruiser come down the driveway. Her parents' thoughts were probably bouncing in all sorts of directions. Probably none of them good.

The moment he stopped the car, she leapt out. Her mother rushed to her, a look of relief etched onto her pretty features.

"I'm okay." She knew they were the words that they would need to hear. "My car has a flat tire, so Mateo brought me home."

Her mother squeezed her into a hug, while her father went to shake Mateo's hand.

"Good to see you, Detective," he said. "Though I wish for once we could meet under less stressful conditions. Thank you for bringing my girl home."

"Happy to do it," Mateo replied.

"Tell us what happened." Her mother's critical gaze scanned over her.

Nina knew, despite her efforts to clean up, she was still a mess. "How about we go inside?" Nina motioned toward the house. "It's a long story. You'll want to sit down."

"That's a good idea," Mateo said. "I'll stay a bit, if that's okay, in case you have any questions."

"Of course." Her mother looped her arm through hers, as if she needed to keep her close.

Truth be told, Nina cherished her mother's presence.

As they walked into the house, she pulled in a breath to try to clear her head and steady her emotions. Some of the earlier shock was wearing off and, for just a moment, she wanted to curl into a ball and sob.

Nope. She couldn't, wouldn't do that. At least, not now. She needed to stay strong for her family. They would be worried enough once they heard about all that had happened. While they would offer her their full support, as they always had, she didn't want to make the situation any harder on them than it was already going to be.

Coco, her chocolate-colored cocker spaniel, greeted them on the other side of the door.

Nina immediately knelt and scooped the dog into her arms. "Hey, there."

Coco pressed her head against Nina's cheek. Calmness instantly swept over her. She loved this girl and seeing her always brought Nina joy.

"Who is this?"

Nina pivoted to look at Mateo. His eyes seemed to light up at the sight of her furry friend. He held out a hand, which the dog eagerly sniffed.

"This is Coco."

Mateo scratched the dog's ears and Coco immediately looked smitten. "Why wasn't she at the park with you?"

"My nephew, Wyatt, has really been missing his mom lately." Nina knew Mateo had worked the case involving Wyatt's mother's murder.

Mateo nodded. "Understandable."

"Coco's a certified therapy dog."

"Really?" Mateo's eyebrows hitched in interest.

"I've wanted a dog for as long as I can remember. When I moved back to Mulberry Creek last year, I started searching rescue organizations. Coco was pulled from a hoarding situation. She was just a puppy, the tiny runt of the litter. The conditions were deplorable. I knew I had to have her. It was love at first sight." She pressed a kiss onto the top of Coco's head. "I knew right away she was something special. I think, maybe because she knew what it was like to come from a miserable situation, she's good at sensing emotions in others. I decided to get her certified and I haven't regretted it."

"Huh. I've heard of therapy dogs," Mateo said. "I've never met one. K-9 officers, sure. We have one on the department. But not therapy dogs. What do you use her for? I mean other than Wyatt?"

"I often bring her to hospice care with me to help soothe the families I work with, only at their request, of course. Sometimes I take her to the Senior Center, or the nursing home, when I volunteer." Nina smiled at the dog affectionately. "It goes without saying she's great with people, really in tune with their emotions. Wyatt adores her. Cassie called this morning to ask if they could borrow her for the day. I couldn't say no. Besides, while I normally do take her to the park with me, it's easier to take photos without her tagging along. Dogs have to be on leashes, understandably. And I'm not quite coordinated enough to maneuver her leash and my camera."

Her mother nodded. "When Cassie heard about the shooting at the park, and that you were there, she thought you might need Coco more than Wyatt. She said to give you her love, but she couldn't stay. The twins are colicky and Eric had his hands full."

"It was sweet of her to bring Coco back." Nina was trying to delay the inevitable conversation, but her mother had reached the end of her patience.

"Tell me," Julia demanded, "how are you, really? I cannot believe that shots were fired at Mulberry Creek Park. It's always been such a quiet, relaxing getaway for us. When I couldn't get you on your phone, I have to say, I started to panic. There are already so many rumors going around, but nothing has been substantiated yet."

"There'll be a press conference," Mateo said. Something like a shooting, especially in a state park, was a big deal. A "critical incident," he had told Nina earlier. "The police chief will be speaking. Probably later this afternoon."

Julia pressed her hand to her heart. "Oh, my."

"Let's sit down." Nina glanced at Mateo and motioned for him to follow, lest he get the notion he should make a hasty retreat before she dropped a verbal bomb on her parents.

They all took seats in the living room. Her parents settled on the sofa, and she and Mateo each took one of the cozy chairs across from them.

"So, the park? The shooter?" Julia's gaze darted between Mateo and Nina. "Did you see him? Were you a good distance away? Were you safe?"

"Well…" Nina hedged.

Mateo gave her a subtle nod of encouragement.

Best to just drop that bomb and get it over with.

"Actually, the shooter happened to be after...me."

Mateo thought it was a good thing Julia was sitting when Nina hit her with the news. If not, she may have collapsed. As Nina's parents listened to her describe her ordeal, her mother looked appropriately horrified. Her father, James, a brawny, recently retired rancher, looked like he was ready to bolt out the door and hunt down the attacker himself.

Mateo sat back in his chair as he let Nina take the lead. Coco sat at her feet. Her head rested on Nina's lap and she stared adoringly at her owner. Nina absently petted the dog, even as she continued to answer her parents' questions.

"I'm sorry, hold up a minute." Julia held a hand in the air as if to halt her daughter's speech, but maybe it was actually to pause a moment to let her mind catch up to Nina's words. She visibly shuddered. James reached out a hand to steady her. "Your *house* blew up?"

"Yes." Nina winced then looked at Mateo as if silently pleading for his help. "It did."

"I understand how disturbing this is to hear." He leaned forward, addressing her parents. He used his calmest, most professional voice. "But we need to focus on what's important here. Nina is *safe*."

"Yes," Julia murmured. "God was watching over her. And *you*."

Had God been watching over him? Mateo supposed He had. It was almost a foreign thought to him these days, to feel watched over, protected by the Creator. A niggling little voice reminded him that God had not been the one to put distance between them.

He cleared his throat, not ready to ponder that right now. Besides, Nina's parents needed answers and reassurance. "I can tell you, the entire Mulberry Creek PD is on this case. We're making it a top priority."

"A shooting in the park of all places." James looked disgusted. Then realization sank in. "Wait a minute. You said he slashed your tires? And he blew up your house. He knows who you are."

Nina winced. "Yes."

"You're being targeted." Julia's eyes widened in alarm. "The shooting in the park? That seems impulsive. But your house? That was premeditated. Intentional."

Yes, it was. Mateo was well aware of that and did not like the implications one bit. He had a hunch that this guy was going to be relentless now that Nina was on his radar. He'd been up against criminals like this before. The only way to stop them was to catch them.

He wasn't going to be the one to tell Nina's parents that she was not going to be safe until this man was behind bars. He knew they were still trying to process all the information that had been thrown at them, but they would figure it out soon enough.

Mateo wasn't even sure if Nina had come to that conclusion yet. She was an intelligent lady and would figure it out sooner rather than later.

Just because she'd survived the explosion did not mean that she was safe.

He glanced at her. The look in her eyes as they latched onto his made it clear that, yes, she had already come to that conclusion. She was well aware that her life was still in danger. He admired her calm and knew it was for her parents' benefit. He had to assume that inside she was quaking. She wasn't going to let her fear show. Not here, not now, at least.

"Mateo, I cannot tell you how grateful I am to you for

taking care of Nina." Julia pulled in a shaky breath. "If anything would have happened to her. I can't even—" She cut herself off and pressed a hand to her lips, as if finishing the sentence was too difficult to bear.

"Yeah, I get it. Losing your child is every parent's worst fear." Mateo inwardly grimaced. He hadn't meant to say that. Hadn't meant to go there. They probably thought he was referring to their oldest daughter, Ella. They would have no way of knowing he'd been referring to his own loss. He was not about to tell them. Instead, he hurried on. "But we're not going to let that happen."

"I don't understand how anyone who knows Nina could want to hurt her." Julia turned to James, who patted her hand.

"It makes no sense." James scowled.

"You're right," Mateo agreed. "He's not rational and that makes him unpredictable. It's likely that little he does will make sense."

He realized too late that that was the wrong thing to say.

"He's not going to stop." Julia's voice was strained and Mateo noticed she squeezed her husband's hand so hard her knuckles turned white. "He's going to keep coming after her."

"Don't you worry," James reassured her. "She'll stay here. We won't let him get close enough to harm her."

Nina bit her lip. Mateo could see how much she hated this. Not for herself, but she hated putting her parents through such grief.

"Promise me." Julia's gaze held Mateo's. "Promise me that you won't let anything happen to my baby girl."

"Mom." Nina shot him an apologetic look. "I'm not Mateo's responsibility."

"Actually, you are," he disagreed. "As a paid officer of the law, it's my job to protect anyone in danger."

As a paid officer of the law? Had he actually said that? Yes, he had.

Why? Because it was easier than admitting she wasn't just anyone. How was it possible that in just one short day, this woman had pressed her way into his heart? Granted, today wasn't the first time he'd met Nina. If he were honest with himself, he'd have to admit he'd admired her fiery spirit when she'd tried to shoo him out of her brother's hospital room after a vigorous round of questioning last fall. She'd been firm yet polite. Professional. Determined. Protective.

Beautiful.

He inwardly winced because that was *not* relevant right now. Nor was it a reason to remember that it had taken him days, weeks maybe, to put that encounter out of his mind. She had made an impression on him that day.

There was no denying he was feeling all sorts of fluttery emotions that he hadn't felt in years. And not so fluttery emotions. Because he also felt a hard determination to keep the attacker from ever getting close enough to hurt her again.

"Promise me," Julia pressed, pulling him back to the moment.

Mateo knew he shouldn't; knew better than to make a promise like that. Yet he wanted nothing more than to keep Nina safe. Even after what they'd been through today, he couldn't say he knew her well. But he knew her *well enough.* Knew that he admired her spunk and respected her coolness under pressure. Knew that looking at her now, all disheveled and vulnerable, yet still undeniably lovely, caused something inside him to stir. The sort of something he hadn't felt for a very long time…attraction toward a woman. And not just a physical attraction because, yes, she was alluring, but it was more than that. She was sweet and caring, and loved her family passionately. And her adorable dog.

"I'll keep her safe." The words flowed from his mouth, solid and strong. "I promise."

He felt that promise all the way down into his soul. In that moment, he knew he would keep Nina safe, or die trying.

FIVE

It had been a long while since Mateo had sat on an overnight protection detail. His duties as a detective often pulled him in other directions. Yet here he sat, in the dark, on the Montgomery's covered front porch, tucked away in the shadows. His shoulder ached something awful. He'd taken a look at it earlier, when he'd gone back to the station for his vehicle and had managed to have a few minutes to himself. It was badly bruised, as he'd suspected, but whatever had pummeled him in the explosion hadn't broken the skin. Regardless, it made leaning back in the chair less than comfortable. Still, this was where he needed to be.

Chief Barsness had only been mildly surprised by the request, but hadn't balked at it.

Mateo could blame the unexpected change in duties on Julia Montgomery, her insistence that he promise to watch over Nina. That would only be a half-truth. It wasn't just because of his promise to her mother that he was sitting there. It was because he didn't want to leave Nina's protection to anyone else.

A ridiculous sentiment, he knew, because in any other situation, he'd trust the other members of the MCPD implicitly. In all honesty, he realized as he sat there in the dark, taking in the sounds of the night—the rustle of the leaves, the chirping of distant frogs—he did trust those on his force, but he'd *wanted* to be there.

Usually at times like this, when it was too still, too calm, his mind would wander to his boys. Tonight, though, his thoughts kept straying to how close he and Nina had come to dying. If she'd flipped the light switch, there would have been an entirely different ending to this situation. For both of them.

A creak cut through the night. The sound, though nearly inaudible, seemed to reverberate through his brain. It sent his senses on high alert. He silently sprang from the Adirondack chair he'd been stationed in. Quickly, quietly, pulling his sidearm, he moved noiselessly across the porch.

If he wasn't mistaken, the sound had come from the back of the house. He knew a screen door off the sunroom led to a cement patio that overlooked the backyard. Was the creaking sound that of rusty hinges? Had someone sneaked past him? Bypassed the front of the house? Perhaps cut through the woods? It was possible as the ranch was surrounded by acres and acres of thick trees.

The Montgomerys knew he was there on patrol and he'd assumed they were all sleeping soundly in their beds. They were counting on him to keep them all safe.

And he would.

He rushed around the side of the house, prepared to take a would-be intruder down. He only hoped that the trespasser hadn't managed to get inside yet. Doubtful, since he knew the Montgomerys had locked up tight. Even if the screen door had opened, he was sure no one could easily breach the entry door that led inside.

As he rounded the side of their home, he stopped in his tracks. Instead of seeing someone trying to break in, as he'd anticipated, he saw someone move away from the house. A small light led the person's steps. It was directed toward the ground, and muted, but to him it looked like an unnecessary beacon.

Why would anyone be leaving the house in the middle of the night? What could they possibly be thinking?

He was certainly going to find out.

He hustled after the person, sure it wasn't an intruder after all, but not holstering his gun just in case. A gentle breeze fluttered the leaves on the trees, making a whispering sound that muffled his footsteps. He glanced over his shoulder, scoping out the yard behind him as best he could in the dark, then he whipped back around, following his quarry.

Mateo was only vaguely familiar with the layout of Big Sky Ranch. Yet the person he was now silently stalking seemed to have a keen sense of awareness as to where they were headed. The light, he now realized, was a flashlight app illuminating the way down a trail. If Mateo was not mistaken, the trail would come out at the main ranch house, the original structure on the property, which was now inhabited by Nina's brother, Eric, and his wife, Cassie.

He shook his head in bewilderment, positive beyond a doubt, that the figure he was quickly gaining on was Nina.

But why? She had seemed afraid earlier. The fact that she was outside, alone, in the middle of the night, was baffling.

What in the world is she doing?

Anger and frustration sizzled up Mateo's spine. He had vowed to keep this woman safe and here she was running through the woods at night. As if she had no regard for her own safety.

"Stop right there." His words sounded hard, cold, as they shot through the night in an undertone only loud enough for her to hear. He was only feet from her now.

She whirled, clapping her hand over her mouth, allowing a whimper to escape as she likely sealed a full-fledged scream inside.

"Mateo." She growled his name under her breath, as if he was the one at fault here. "You scared the ever-loving daylights out of me."

He closed the distance between them, slipped his fingers around her bicep, fully intending to tow her back to her parents' home. Back to safety. "You're fortunate that's all that happened to you. There are far worse things than being scared. Like dying."

He gave her arm a gentle tug and was surprised he was met with resistance.

"I know." She kept her voice low, as he had, as if they both feared danger was lurking in the darkness. It very well might be. "That's exactly why I need to get out of here."

"Where do you plan on going?" He glanced around, feeling as if they were targets standing there in the darkness. Nina must've felt the same because she turned off the beam of light she'd been using.

"Where? Anywhere but here," she said grimly.

"You think it's wise to leave the safety of the ranch?"

"Yes." The single word held so much weight. "Mateo, this person shot at us. Then blew up my house. What if he comes after me here? I can't risk him hurting my parents. My brothers and their families live on this property. Eric and Cassie just had twins and they have Wyatt. Seth and Holly have Chloe and a baby on the way. I can't be here with them. I can't put them at risk. If anything, anything at all, happened to them, I would never forgive myself. Please tell me you understand."

Understand that level of guilt? He understood more

clearly than he cared to admit. He wouldn't tell her that, though.

"Exactly what were you going to do?" he demanded.

She shifted the hefty camping pack she wore.

For a moment, he thought she wasn't going to answer.

"Eric just bought an old beater of a ranch truck for doing chores. He keeps a spare key in the kitchen at Mom and Dad's. I swiped it out of the drawer. My plan is a bit hazy at the moment because I haven't had a chance to come up with something solid. Quite frankly, my only thought right now is that I need to get away."

"You were just going to take off? No warning? Just disappear?" He huffed in annoyance. "Don't you think that would scare your parents to death?"

She let out a matching huff of annoyance. "I left a note."

A note.

He scraped a hand over his face. Right. He could just imagine how well a note would go over with Julia and James.

"I get that you're scared, but this harebrained plan... running through the woods alone at night, stealing a truck and taking off without knowing exactly what you're going to do, is just the sort of thing that might get you killed."

"Harebrained?" Nina's voice held an edge. "And I wasn't *stealing* the truck. I was *borrowing* it. I would have come up with a plan as soon as I got far enough away from my family to think clearly."

It was obvious she was mad.

Maybe even a little hurt.

He couldn't think about that too much right now. He wasn't anything too happy either. If she had disappeared on his watch...well, he didn't want to think about it. He was grateful for the squeaky screen door because, other than that, Nina had the stealth of a cat. He wouldn't have realized she'd run off until she'd torn out of the driveway in her brother's truck.

"We can't stand out in the open arguing like this." His eyes zoomed around as he realized just how far away from the house they were, closer to Eric's place than her parents'. Standing out here felt all kinds of wrong. He didn't like being in the open. Certainly didn't like Nina out here, even if he was armed. "We need to get back. If you really think you need to leave—"

"I do."

He didn't see any point in arguing with her. She was stubborn. More than that, she might be right. Helping her to disappear for a while suddenly seemed like the best option. Not necessarily for her safety, but definitely for that of her family. He would've recommended leaving town before, but had assumed she'd be opposed to the idea of leaving.

"Okay then, this time we'll be smart about it. We'll make a plan to get you someplace safe. Somewhere far away from your family." He was already flipping through possibilities in his mind.

"Fine." Her tone was terse, but then she seemed to soften. "I'm sorry, Mateo. You may not think I made the best choice just now, but I'm just worried about my family. If you have a better plan, I'm open to it."

"You should have discussed this with me sooner."

"I didn't really get the chance. My parents were hovering. Also, I was afraid you'd tell me I should stay."

"Let's get back inside for now. We'll go from there."

This time when he tugged her arm, she didn't resist.

They traipsed back up the path through the woods. Neither said a word. Without a light to guide them, they moved slowly, but he wasn't willing to take an unnecessary risk.

Guilt niggled at him. He'd come down hard on her. Too hard. It was clear she was acting out of selflessness. Love for her family had motivated her. Yet that did nothing to mitigate the danger she was in. Walking outside at night, creeping through the woods, was reckless in his eyes.

Nina walked silently beside him. Not sulkily, but contrite, if he wasn't mistaken.

An apology was on the tip of his tongue. Before he could utter the words, a flash up ahead snagged his attention. Not the same sort of light that had emanated from Nina's phone. No, this light flickered.

Nina grasped his forearm, her grip ironclad, indicating she had noticed as well. He appreciated the fact that she didn't utter a word, seemingly understanding that danger lay ahead and, right now, they had the element of surprise on their side.

"Stay here," he whispered, his mouth right next to her ear.

He darted forward, tugging his arm from her grip.

The light up ahead glimmered and seemed to glow, vaguely illuminating the silhouette of the man holding the flame. His arm rose, hoisting the burning object higher.

"Freeze!" Mateo shouted. "MCPD! Stop where you are."

The man faltered for a split second then whipped the burning object toward the house. An explosion of flames erupted when the Molotov cocktail fell short of its target. Instead of being hurled through the window, it erupted on the Adirondack chair Mateo had vacated to chase after Nina. The piece of furniture went up in a whoosh of flame.

Nina let out a shriek of anger and fear.

The figure took off running.

"Get your parents out of the house!" Mateo shot off the

warning before giving chase. He called for backup on his shoulder radio even as he ran. Then he prayed.

Please, God...watch over Nina's family. Get them out of the house safely.

He had to trust that Nina would do just that because he desperately wanted to catch this guy.

The night was inky-dark and the man had dressed in black. Though Mateo gave a valiant effort to catch the perp, dodging through the thick brush, trying to make out the figure in the darkness, listening for any hint of snapping branches, it wasn't long before he realized that his effort was in vain.

Mateo stopped running and leaned against a tree, more for camouflage than anything else. Ears straining, he only heard the natural sounds of the night that he'd been listening to on the porch earlier. The woods weren't familiar to him, so it didn't make sense to push forward. He had to assume the attacker was running blindly as well.

After a moments' pause, he pushed away from the tree because he suddenly feared the guy would backtrack and launch a sneak attack on Nina and her family. He thought it unlikely, but decided it was better to head back to the house than to take any chances.

When he arrived, he found Nina and her mother standing in the driveway, huddled together. The porch light shone down, lighting up the mass of charred wood that had been a chair.

James, her father, held a garden hose that spouted water on the remainder of the smoldering furniture. The porch had major damage, but the house seemed to have been spared.

A cruiser tore down the driveway, lights flashing in warning but sirens silent, just as Mateo strode out of the woods.

Officer Baker, a rookie, tossed the door open and leapt from the vehicle. His gaze immediately locked with Mateo's. "Sir? What do you have?"

Mateo headed for the young officer. "The suspect tossed a Molotov cocktail. He missed the window. The damage appears to be contained to the front porch." He eyed the smoking mess. "I gave chase, but lost him in the woods, so I came back. I was concerned he might backtrack."

The officer's gaze flitted around. "I'll do a perimeter check."

"Good idea." Mateo strode toward Nina and her family when the officer took off. "Everyone okay?"

"We're fine. I pounded on the door to alert my parents, then I grabbed the hose until Dad took over." Nina untangled herself from her mother's embrace. "The attacker got away."

It wasn't a question and it certainly wasn't an accusation. Yet Mateo felt a sting of disappointment all the same.

"Yeah. He got away."

Again.

Nina could feel the frustration emanating off Mateo. She didn't like that he seemed to be so hard on himself. His gaze still scanned the yard, completely on guard and still in protection mode.

"You scared him off," she said. "Stopped him from hurting anyone. Thank you."

She felt a niggling stab of guilt. If she hadn't run off, hadn't given Mateo a reason to trek after her through the woods, he would have been sitting in a prime position to catch the man who had thrown the homemade fireball. He would have been where he'd intended to be.

"Yes." James finally gave up his effort with the hose. The

fire was out and even the smoldering had dwindled. "I second my daughter's sentiment. Thank you. You saved us tonight from what would have surely been something disastrous."

"Just doing my job."

"Going above and beyond," Julia chimed in.

As if their thoughts were in unison, and very likely they were, both of her parents turned to face her.

Julia frowned. "What were *you* doing outside? It's the middle of the night. Someone is after you. What in the world were you thinking?"

Nina knew there was no sense in denying what she'd been up to. Her parents hadn't found the note on the kitchen table yet and she could hardly race inside to tear it up without raising suspicion. Besides, her plans hadn't changed. Quite the contrary. After this latest attack, she was even more convinced that she was doing the right thing.

"I'm leaving." Her statement hung in the air, unanswered, as if her parents couldn't process what she was saying. "Right now. I'm leaving the ranch. It's not safe for me to be here. Not safe for me, and worse, not safe for my family."

"You don't need to worry about us." Her father sounded confused by the sentiment. "We want you here. We want to help protect you."

"But I *am* worried." Nina's gaze darted between her parents. "I worry about you. But I also worry about my nieces and nephews. You can't tell me that you wouldn't be devastated if something happened to them."

"Of course we would," Julia said with a frown, "but—"

"There's no point in arguing," Nina cut in. "I couldn't bear it if something happened to them. After tonight, there's no denying he knows I'm here. Do you think he's going to stop? He's been relentless so far. I can't take that chance."

Her parents exchanged a pained look.

Her mother sighed. "As much as I hate to admit it, perhaps you're right. I'm worried about everyone's safety, but most of all, I'm worried about *you* since you're his target."

"Exactly." Nina was relieved her mother saw things her way. "*I'm* the target. If I move on, hopefully he won't come back."

"Okay—" her mother nodded "—we'll pack our bags right now. Your father and I will take you somewhere far from here."

What? No.

That was not what Nina had had in mind at all. If her parents were with her, they would still be in danger. She shot a frantic look Mateo's way, hoping he would also think it was a terrible idea. Thankfully, he seemed to agree.

"I don't think that's wise," he said. "You might just be putting yourselves in danger, along with Nina."

James huffed. "I'm hardly going to send my daughter off on her own and hope for the best."

"Of course." Mateo's tone was conciliatory, calming. "That's why I think it's best if I take Nina somewhere. I'm equipped to protect her."

Her parents shared a long look.

"I don't like this at all," James finally said. "I don't like any of this. But I don't think we have any other option."

"Where would you go?" Julia demanded.

"I have a few places in mind. I think it's best if I don't say where." Mateo's gaze swung between her parents. "The less you know, the better."

Nina nodded, silently letting him know she agreed.

Everything was happening so fast, her world seemingly spinning out of control. She was relieved that he was willing to take charge.

"What do you think?" Mateo directed the question at Nina. "I've got a few options. Places that are off the beaten path. Somewhere no one would think to look for you. Obviously, I haven't worked out the details, or even decided yet which place might be best, but I've got a pretty good idea."

To be honest, she wasn't entirely sure what she thought. She hadn't had enough time to really wrap her head around the suggestion. On the other hand, he had a plan, which was more than she had. Furthermore, it got her away from her family and, therefore, would hopefully get them out of harm's way.

"Let's do it," she said.

Less than fifteen minutes later, they were loaded into Mateo's SUV. Her mother had packed enough food to last them days, ensuring they wouldn't need to stop anywhere. Nina had her backpack loaded with clothes Holly had lent her. She and her sister-in-law were typically close to the same size, though now Holly was hugely pregnant. She had given Nina free reign over her wardrobe since Nina had lost all of her clothing in the explosion.

Officer Baker had checked in, letting Mateo know that he hadn't seen any sign of the intruder. The man had gotten away somehow. Perhaps he'd hiked in and had hidden a vehicle somewhere.

Coco let out a sigh of contentment from the back seat where Nina had buckled her in to her doggy car seat. Her original intention was to leave the dog behind, but once they'd gone in the house to pack up the food Julia had insisted on, Coco had made it clear she wasn't pleased with that idea.

So here they were. Mateo, Nina and Coco, cruising down the back roads in the dead of night.

Nina prayed that they were heading toward safety.

SIX

Nina was pleasantly surprised by what Mateo had warned her was a hunting "shack." It was small and rustic, but it also had indoor plumbing and other amenities that she would never take for granted.

Like electricity and semicomfy furniture. There was a fridge, stove, and essentially a fully functioning kitchen. It was far from fancy, but she'd been picturing a ramshackle place with an outhouse at best.

It was far enough out of town that it was private, surrounded by trees, with the nearest house miles away. Yet close enough they could drive back and forth easily while doing some investigating. Still, it had taken them nearly an hour to arrive tonight because Mateo had insisted on a roundabout route to be sure they were not followed.

The loft held a single bedroom, which Mateo insisted Nina and Coco take. There was a futon in the small living area downstairs. Mateo assured her it was perfect for him. It would station him near the front door and windows on the off chance that someone had tracked them there.

She was dragging by the time she lugged her backpack inside. Mateo had a duffel bag, his go-bag, which he kept in his SUV so that he wouldn't have to stop by his place for anything. He carried in the generous food supply from Julia while Nina settled in upstairs.

Coco trotted down the steep wooden staircase after Nina, who yawned hugely, after checking out the loft.

Mateo glanced up from where he was stashing the last container in the refrigerator. The cooler stuffed with every ice pack her mother owned rested at his feet. He looked as fatigued as she felt.

"All settled?" he asked.

"Yes." She moved to the well-worn chair and dropped down, her body feeling heavy with fatigue. "What's the game plan?"

He dropped onto the futon and arched a brow. "Game plan?"

"You know what I mean." Coco plopped her bottom at Nina's feet and placed her chin on Nina's knee. She stroked the dog's long, silky ears lovingly. "We're not going to just hang out here, waiting for this guy to be caught, are we?"

"Not exactly." Mateo leaned forward. "I want to go over some details of your life. I have questions about your job, your volunteer work. The people you hang out with."

She nodded. "I understand. I've been wracking my brain, trying to figure out how I could possibly know this man. But I've lived in Mulberry Creek most of my life. What if it's someone I knew as far back as high school?"

"Always a possibility. Recognizing you is one thing. But who would recognize your vehicle?"

Nina's eyes widened as she realized what Mateo was getting at. "It would have to be someone I've been in contact with recently. I've only had that vehicle two, maybe three, months. I drove an old beater through nursing school. When I started working in the ER, I worked mostly night shifts and slept most days. My schedule was all over the place and I didn't have time to look for something new. I didn't actually get my vehicle until I started working for hospice."

"Good." Mateo nodded and looked pleased. "That narrows the suspects down a bit. We don't have to go all the way back to high school because it's not just *you* they recognized but your vehicle."

"Right." She yawned again.

"The thing is, it's kind of a flashy color. The kind that gets noticed."

Nina wrinkled her nose, almost apologetically. "I wanted four-wheel drive. I need something reliable to get around because hospice sometimes brings me to places out in the country. You know what Montana winters can be like. Cherry red wasn't my top choice but the price was right. The color *does* stand out."

Mateo chuckled. "I'm not criticizing your choice. I'm just saying it's noticeable and makes sense someone connected it to you. I also noticed you had a decal on the back window that says 'Blessed' and, while it's subtle, it would still be an identifier."

"Makes me kind of wish I still had my old beater," she muttered. "No one ever paid attention to that."

"It's barely past daybreak," Mateo said. "I don't think either of us got a wink of sleep last night. What do you say we both get some rest? I think it would do us some good to sleep. We'll be able to come at this with clearer heads. Besides, we don't know what the next few days, maybe even weeks, will bring. I, for one, want to be at the top of my game."

"Me, too." Nina fought the urge to yawn. Again. "Sleep is sounding way too appealing right now."

Mateo cocked his head toward Coco. "What kind of guard dog is she?"

"A useless one." Nina chuckled then sobered. "Everyone is her friend. She's well trained and doesn't typically bark, not even at strangers. But do you think we need a guard dog?"

"No." Mateo sounded positive. "I can guarantee we weren't followed. Not only did I take precautions, but there was simply no traffic on the back roads we took. The man I borrowed this place from is a retired sheriff, a friend of my dad's. He won't tell a soul that we're here."

She felt herself relax at Mateo's obvious confidence. She didn't think he'd say they were safe if they weren't. Sure, she knew there were no guarantees, but she understood that in his professional opinion they were as safe as they could get.

For now.

"Was your dad in law enforcement?" she asked, curious about his family.

"He was. Worked as a deputy until he retired several years ago." Mateo motioned around the cabin, which Nina no longer thought of as a shack. "I spent some time here when I was younger, joining them on hunting trips. Not once did we see another soul out this way. It's a good place for us to hide out for a while."

Satisfied with his answer, she rose from her chair. "Coco, let's go. Get some rest, Mateo."

"Will do."

With great effort, Nina climbed the staircase again. She went straight to the bed in the small loft, flopped down without bothering to peel back the covers—only vaguely aware of Coca taking the liberty to snuggle in beside her—and fell into blissful slumber.

She awoke several hours later, feeling refreshed but absolutely starving. She stretched and gave herself a moment to gather her wits about her. The memory of the events of the day before came crashing back.

She sucked in a pained breath at the realization that her house, all of her belongings, were gone. Her heart thudded painfully as she recalled the explosion, the blaze. Then she reminded herself that it could have been so much worse. Her family, as far as she knew, was safe.

When it came down to it, that's all that really mattered.

She swung her legs over the bed. Coca stirred beside her.

"Did you have a good nap, sweet girl?"

The dog yawned.

Clattering from downstairs grabbed Nina's attention. She realized then that a savory aroma filled the air.

She also realized that Mateo was awake.

If he'd even slept.

A quick glance at her watch let her know it was well after lunchtime. She was surprised she'd slept so long considering all that was going on. Then again, she'd been utterly exhausted. Both physically and emotionally. So she was going to choose to give herself some grace.

She hustled down the staircase and found Mateo in the kitchen.

"Is that my mom's stew I smell?"

Mateo glanced over his shoulder and flashed her a grin. "It is. It sure came in handy that your mom had all those frozen meals. I popped the biscuits in the oven to warm. Everything should be ready in just a few minutes."

Nina's stomach growled.

He chuckled. "I can relate."

Coco whimpered.

Mateo stepped away from the stove. "I'll take her out."

"I'll set the table." She easily found what she was looking

for in the limited cupboard space. By the time she had the table set and food set out, Mateo and Coco were back inside.

They took the only two seats at the tiny table.

Nina lowered her head to say a silent prayer. She was aware that Mateo waited for her to finish before dishing himself up.

"Did you sleep?" Nina took a roll and spread a thin layer of butter on it.

"A little." He set the soup ladle back in the pot.

He hadn't looked at her when he'd said it, leaving her to wonder how "little" was little. She knew he hadn't slept nearly as long as she had, but he did look more refreshed.

They ate in silence for a while, both of them clearly famished. Nina hadn't had an appetite the night before when she'd sat through dinner with her worried parents. She'd skipped breakfast this morning in lieu of the nap she'd just awakened from. Now her appetite seemed to be making up for a few missed meals.

"Your mom is a great cook." Mateo set his spoon down. "I'm pretty mediocre myself. Do you take after her?"

"I try. I do like to cook, but there's nothing that beats Mom's home cooking." She swirled her spoon through the stew. "Do you have any information to share?"

"Officer Hughes confirmed that none of your pictures show this guy's face."

"I'm not surprised. I didn't think any of them would be useful."

Mateo's phone buzzed. He grabbed it off the table and read the incoming message with a frown.

"Something wrong?"

"Seems we've hit a bit of a roadblock already. Officer Rollins called earlier and now he's touching base again."

"What kind of roadblock?"

"We have to start this investigation somewhere, so we decided to start with one of the places you volunteer. He went to the Senior Center with pictures of the items found in the lockbox. We had all of the photos put into a few three-ring binders. I have one—picked it up from the station last night when I got my vehicle—because we're hoping it'll be useful when interviewing people. Rollins wasn't getting any answers, so he mentioned your name, hoping it would loosen some tongues if they knew it would help you out." Mateo grimaced. "Apparently that backfired. One of the visitors got it into her head that you were in trouble. And not in trouble like being shot at, but in trouble like you had done something wrong and might be headed to jail."

Nina's eyes widened. "What?"

"It seems that a Mrs. Marjorie Wallace told him she had warned you but you wouldn't listen." His brow creased. "Just what is she referring to? What did she warn you about? You don't really seem like a troublemaker to me."

Nina pressed a hand against her forehead and groaned. "Mrs. Wallace is always telling me that Coco is going to get me in trouble. According to her, people cannot bring pets into public buildings. I've explained that Coco is a service dog. She wears a vest when we're working. I even showed Marjorie the certificate we earned. But she's very old school and is always telling me dogs belong outside. She insists I'm violating all sorts of health codes."

"Even if she thinks you're at fault, it seems she has your back. Sounds like she was pretty riled up on your behalf. She's determined not to speak with Officer Rollins. And apparently has convinced the others not to as well."

"That's not surprising." Nina pushed away her empty bowl and leaned back in her chair. "She has a very commanding personality."

"Officer Hughes offered to give it a try. Maybe she can make a visit when Mrs. Wallace isn't there."

"She's there daily," Nina said. "And believe me, even if she isn't there, she'd be sure to get the word out. The only way you're going to get anyone to look at those photos and give you any information, is if I go there myself. I need to convince them I'm not in trouble. At least, not the way they suspect."

"I don't think so."

"Why not?" Nina frowned at Mateo but she was sure she could guess the answer. "I'll be safe if I'm with you. Obviously, you should lead the questioning, but I know how this group can be. Very stubborn once they have their minds made up. I'm going to have to convince them it's okay to share if they know something."

She knew how members of the Senior Center liked to talk, at least, under the right circumstances. She was willing to try anything if there was a possibility it would help them find the attacker. There was no doubt that the confrontation at the park was already big news in their town. People would be hungry for information and, for once, the gossip mill could be an asset.

"All right." Mateo pushed away from the table. "I'll get these dishes done. Then I don't see what a quick unannounced visit could hurt. If we get answers, it would be worth it."

Nina leapt to her feet. "I'll wash. You can dry."

In no time at all they were in Mateo's Tahoe, headed back to Mulberry Creek with Coco once again buckled into the backseat. The drive passed quickly as Mateo and Nina made small talk. She suspected he was trying to put her at ease. He needn't worry; there was something about him that was calming. He held an unpretentious air of confidence. She felt safe with him. And she was more than a little intrigued by him. He asked questions about her life, to find out more for his investigation, she was sure. But it didn't feel like he was prying.

By the time they hit the edge of town, Nina realized she hadn't been able to ask *him* a single question. She wanted to know more about him, and it wasn't just because he was the man protecting her. She wanted to know more about him as a person, not a detective.

"I've been thinking." Mateo tapped his fingers on the steering wheel. "It might be worthwhile to stop at Junkin' Treasures."

"I've heard of that. Is it an antique store?"

He turned his blinker on, routing them toward the downtown area. "Pawn shop. I know the owner, Jimmy. He's usually pretty helpful. I'd like to see if he's familiar with any of the items in the binder we put together. I know they weren't stolen from him, but he'd be able to give me an idea of what some of the items are worth. Or maybe this guy has tried to move some of the pieces through Jimmy's store. Not likely, but it's possible."

He pulled up in front of a large brick building. "This is it. Let's see if we can get some information."

Nina had never been in a pawn shop before, yet it was about as she'd expected it to be. A musty smell hung in the air. Rows of overcrowded shelves were lined with goods, possibly even some hidden treasures. A local rock station was being piped in through speakers in the ceiling. And the place looked like it could use a good cleaning.

What she had not expected was the way the proprietor's face lit up when she and Mateo walked through the door. Somehow, she had a hunch the enormous smile the guy wore was not for her.

"Mateo! My man!" Jimmy ducked around the side of the counter and strode straight for them. "Long time no see." He held up a hand, clearly waiting for a high-five.

For a moment, Nina wondered if Mateo would leave him hanging. Then he gave Jimmy's hand a powerful albeit somewhat awkward smack. Nina realized casual high-fives were not Mateo's thing.

"Good to see you, Jimmy." Mateo shifted the binder he held. "Listen, I'm wondering if you could help me and my friend, Nina, out."

"Hi, Jimmy." Nina smiled at the man and wiggled her fingers in a wave of greeting.

"Nice to meet you. Any friend of this guy is a friend of mine."

"Oh, really?" Nina asked, arching a brow. "You must think pretty highly of him."

"Yup, sure do." Jimmy nodded for emphasis. "Did he tell you what he did for me?"

Nina cut a quick glance to Mateo. His expression was that of stoic patience. Then she shook her head. "He didn't mention anything."

"This guy here—" Jimmy jabbed a finger in Mateo's direction "—pretty much saved my business. You see, a few years ago, I was having trouble with someone shoplifting. My most expensive items kept going missing, but even with security cameras, I couldn't catch the guy. Turns out the thief was an employee of mine. He'd made himself a key and snuck in at night, would mess with my cameras, and take off with the goods. I never would've suspected him. Trusted him like a friend. But our guy here came in and rooted out the scheme in no time."

Mateo cleared his throat and lifted the binder.

"Sure. Right." Jimmy rubbed his hands together in anticipation. "What do you got?"

Mateo motioned at the counter and Jimmy nodded, leading the way.

"I'm not sure what I have exactly." Mateo set the binder down but didn't open it. "I suspect stolen items. I'm wondering if you could help me get an idea of what these items are worth."

"Sure thing."

Mateo slid it Jimmy's way. "Have at it."

Jimmy opened the binder. He went through it slowly, meticulously, studying each page without saying a word. Yet the way his brow creased in concentration led Nina to believe he was taking this task quite seriously.

After several long minutes, he flipped back to a page in the middle. He tapped his finger on the photo depicting the collection of stamps. "I remember these."

"Are you sure it was that exact set?" Mateo asked.

"Positive." Jimmy nodded emphatically. "This is a unique collection of antique postage stamps, pre-Civil War era, and valuable. A guy came in, quite a while ago, asking me if I was interested. It's not the type of thing I typically sell, but I was willing to haggle a bit. We couldn't come to an agreement on price. Truth be told, I got the impression he didn't really want to sell. I think he just wanted to get an appraisal out of me."

Nina's heart skittered and she wanted to jiggle all of Jimmy's information free. She shifted a glance at Mateo. He looked a million times calmer than she felt.

"Do you recall the guy's name?" Mateo asked.

Jimmy scratched his head with one finger. His brows puckered. "Nope. I don't." He paused, then turned around and motioned to the mess behind him. "I took his name down. I'm pretty sure it's here somewhere."

Nina scanned the space. There were notebooks, receipt books, loose sheets of paper, and a plethora of odds and ends scattered across the space.

"Then again, could be I brought it back to my office," Jimmy admitted. "I don't keep that quite as tidy as I keep this area."

He thought this was tidy? Oh, goodness. Nina couldn't even imagine how disastrous his office could be.

"Can you give me a description?" Mateo asked.

"Older fella. Maybe close to eighty. Walked a little hunched over. I remember, I had a real nice hand-carved cane at the time. I thought maybe he'd be interested in it, but he didn't take too kindly to my suggestion. He was a cantankerous sort. Tried to talk me into giving him more than what the value was. A guy's gotta have some room for profit, so, like I said, we couldn't cut a deal."

Nina bit her lip. She didn't want to blurt out the obvious. Close to eighty? That couldn't be their guy. So how did he tie in?

"How long ago was this?" Mateo asked.

"Oh, a good three, four, months ago. He gave me his name and number in case I changed my mind. I knew I wouldn't—" Jimmy shrugged "—but I don't throw much away. Never know when you're going to need something. His information is around here somewhere."

Would he ever find the guy's number in that mess? Nina wondered and then winced at the uncharitable speculation. This could be organized chaos, as far as she knew.

"Jimmy, it would be real helpful if you could remember the gentleman's name. More helpful still if you could track down his number."

"I can sure try," Jimmy agreed amicably enough. "I keep thinking I need to come up with some sort of filing system, but just haven't had the time. Guess now would be a good time to work on that."

"I'd appreciate it," Mateo said.

"As for the value of the items, I'd say we're looking at close to a hundred grand. That's a high-end Rolex and, as I mentioned, the stamps are worth a good deal, not to mention the coins. The thing is, there's lots of jewelry there. Might be that no one would be interested in, say, that gold locket. But looks to me that it's pure gold. There are companies that buy that sort of thing, melt it down, and give you a fair price for it. Places you can find on the internet, even."

Mateo nodded slowly. "That would make these items almost impossible to trace once our guy decided to part with them."

"Yup."

Mateo grabbed the binder. "We'll let you get back to work."

He nudged Nina toward the door. She waved a goodbye to Jimmy. He grinned back, but then turned and immediately began sorting through papers. It looked like he was a man of his word.

They exited the building and Mateo hustled her to his SUV, parked right outside the pawn shop.

"That's not our guy that he was describing." Mateo's words echoed Nina's thoughts as he opened her door for her while scanning the sidewalk. "But whoever he is, it's possible he has information. If he was trying to sell the stamps to Jimmy then maybe he sold them to someone else."

"If our attacker bought everything fair and square, why would he be willing to kill over the items?"

"I agree, it doesn't make sense." Mateo paused thoughtfully. "I hope Jimmy comes up with something for us. The sooner, the better."

Mateo hadn't been certain that allowing Nina to visit the Senior Center was a wise idea, but they hadn't had a lot of other options if they wanted to start getting some answers. His opinion on that changed when he escorted Nina through the door.

The place was bustling with activity. The open space was full of tables and the tables were full of people. At the back of the room, he spotted what looked like an ice cream bar. A long table held large tubs of ice cream. Smaller bowls with nuts, fruits and candies were beside it. At the end was a variety of syrups and whipped cream.

"Today is the ice cream social. I forgot about that." Nina shrugged. "On the bright side, with all of these people here, hopefully one of them will know something."

It seemed as if everyone in the place swiveled to see who had arrived once the door whooshed open.

A spry elderly woman with unnaturally red hair jumped up from her seat. She scurried over to Nina with the agility of a teenager.

"Goodness, girl! What are you doing here?" She pulled Nina into a quick hug. When she released her, she scowled at Coco, who had taken a seat next to Nina's feet. The dog wore a vest with the words Therapy Dog inscribed on it. "Did you come for the ice cream? Oh, you shouldn't have that mutt in here. I told you she'd bring trouble. She shouldn't be around the food." The woman's eyes zipped around and she whispered, "A cop was here looking for you."

"I heard," Nina whispered back. Then louder, added, "That was just a misunderstanding."

"It's about that dog, isn't it? I warned you."

The woman, Marjorie Wallace, Mateo was sure, scowled at him then.

"And who are you?" she demanded.

"This is Detective Bianchi," Nina said.

"Detective?" Marjorie scowled. "That seems a bit excessive for violating a health code."

Mateo remained silent as Nina spent the next several minutes explaining that she, herself, was not *in* trouble. But rather, she'd *faced* a bit of trouble. She spoke freely of being attacked in the park.

By the time she was done with her story, a crowd had gathered around. A few dozen older citizens of Mulberry Creek, who all looked as ravenous for news as they did for their ice cream, leaned in to listen.

"I heard about that," one gentleman said. "It was in the news. Been a lot of talk about it yesterday and today." He scooped up his melted treat and shoved a big bite in his mouth.

Mateo wondered if it was wise that Nina admit she was the one in the park but then realized it was too late to take it back. Besides, the attacker already knew who she was, and in a town this small, it was likely to get out anyway.

"You see," Nina said, "I could really use your help. We're trying to track down my attacker. We're hoping you could look over some photos, see if anything looks familiar. We don't know that these items are the reason behind my attack, but we have to start somewhere."

And with that simple explanation, the gathering of ice cream eaters readily agreed.

Even though Nina had told Mateo she would let him head the questioning, it turned out that she had a knack for getting this lively group of people talking.

Many of them commented on the items in the binder. Some were sure they'd seen some of the objects before and then decided they'd maybe seen a similar item before. Or maybe they'd owned something just like it in the past.

When all was said and done, they'd had a whole lot of conversation, but not one comment had resulted in anything he'd take as a substantial clue. There was a lot of interest in the binder and Nina's story. And when it became clear they weren't going to get anywhere, he decided it was time to move along.

He gave Nina's arm a gentle nudge.

She glanced up from a conversation about a brooch in the binder. Everyone thought it was pretty, but no one had seen it before. Mateo didn't need to say a word. She understood by the look he gave her that it was time to go.

"It was lovely to see you all." She stood and pushed in her chair. "I sincerely thank you for trying to help. But I think it's time for us to be on our way."

"You be careful, young lady." Marjorie looked at Coco. "Maybe you should get yourself a bigger dog. An attack dog. Something that can protect you."

"Thank you, Marjorie." Nina gave Coco's leash a gentle tug and the dog got to her feet. "I appreciate your concern."

"Thank you all for your time," Mateo said. "If any of you think of anything that could relate to the case, please give the police department a call."

He gently took Nina by the elbow and led her to the door. Not because she needed the prodding, but because he suspected that this lively group would waylay her departure if given a chance.

Nina blew out a sigh as they exited the building. "I was hoping someone would recognize something."

Mateo barely heard her. Someone—a man dressed in

torn jeans, a ball cap pulled low over his face—was lurking around his SUV. Mateo watched as he lifted the windshield wiper and stuffed something under it. A threatening note?

Was this their guy?

"Go back inside. Now." He gave Nina a gentle shove toward the building. Then he took off down the sidewalk. The guy spotted him, whirled and began to run like his life depended upon it.

Had this guy done something other than mess with his windshield wiper? Thoughts of Nina's burning house came to mind and he wondered if a car bomb was a possibility. Or a tracking device.

"Stop!" Mateo shouted.

Several people on the sidewalk darted out of the way as the chase continued. The guy dodged people as he ran. He nearly knocked down an elderly couple—maybe on their way to the ice cream social—who righted themselves as Mateo sped by.

He looked over his shoulder once to be sure Nina had complied with his request. She was no longer on the sidewalk. That glance almost cost him the chase as the guy ducked down an alley. But Mateo caught a glimpse of him and tore down the potholed path after him.

"Stop!" he shouted. "Police!"

To his surprise, the runner skidded to a halt. Something a perp almost never did. The kid—Mateo now realized this guy was probably college age—spun around. His hands flew up in the air and his eyes bulged in fear.

"I'm sorry! I'm sorry!" he sputtered. "I didn't mean to do anything wrong."

Mateo quickly closed the distance between them. He had his hand on his weapon, but the kid didn't appear to be armed, so he didn't draw it. "Why did you run?"

The guy blinked at him. "Because you started chasing me. It was just reflex, I guess."

"What's your name?"

"Tucker. Tucker Holden, sir."

"What were you doing to my Tahoe?"

The kid looked around frantically. Mateo realized a crowd was beginning to form behind them. He heard sirens nearing and assumed Nina had called for backup.

"I was just…" Tucker looked miserable. "I saw you and Nina pull up together. I volunteer at the Senior Center and I was just finishing my shift. I was leaving a note for Nina."

"What kind of note?"

"Just a note of support. Nina's always doing nice things for other people." He scrubbed both hands over his face.

Mateo wasn't sure what to make of this guy.

Was he telling the truth?

Or was Tucker Holden, if that was really his name, a would-be cold-blooded killer?

As Mateo's backup arrived and began to swarm the alley, he hoped they'd have an answer soon.

SEVEN

Nina pushed around the noodles on her dinner plate. She typically loved her mother's casseroles, but her stomach had been in knots ever since Tucker had been arrested. She knew him, but felt they had only recently transitioned from acquaintances to friends. Their volunteer paths crossed on occasion. She hadn't seen him at the center today, as he'd been back in the kitchen trying to keep up with all the dirty dishes.

"No appetite?" Mateo guessed. "I know it's not that the food is bad, because this is delicious."

"I can't stop thinking about Tucker. Do you think he's the guy?"

A storm was brewing and thunder rumbled in the distance. The day had turned dark and dreary, matching Nina's current mood.

Mateo set his fork down. "I think the fact that he lied about his whereabouts during the time of the attack in the park raises a major red flag."

Yes, it did, Nina knew. Tucker had been brought in for questioning. When asked, he had said he was working during the time of the attack. Checking in at the Good Stuff Café, with owner Sal Goodman, had been easy enough. Sal had verified that Tucker had *not* been working.

"He said he panicked."

"That is what he said." Mateo's tone was wry. "He also used that excuse for the reason he took off running."

She tilted her head, studying Mateo's unreadable expression. "You don't believe him?"

"I don't want to speculate. I like to look at facts. He has a connection to you. He's roughly the size of the guy who chased us through the park. He lied regarding his whereabouts. When questioned again, he said he was fly fishing, but we can't corroborate that, either."

"Yet."

"Right." Mateo nodded. "Then there's the fact that apparently he's had an unrequited crush on you."

Nina groaned and put her face in her hands. "I had no idea."

This particular nugget of information had come from Marjorie Wallace. Seemingly, Tucker had confided in Marjorie as the pair had become chummy over their love for Monopoly. When Marjorie had found out Tucker had been taken in for questioning, she'd tracked Mateo down at the station to tell him.

While the woman was hoping the admission would help Tucker, it also gave him motive. Could he be upset with Nina for turning him down multiple times? It seemed excessive, but Mateo told Nina he'd seen far stranger cases. Maybe being turned down, paired with having his box full of belongings confiscated, had pushed him over the edge.

"He asked me to go to the Fall Festival at church last year." Nina pushed her plate away because there was no point in pretending she was able to eat. "And there was a dance at the Senior Center that volunteers were encouraged to attend. I declined both because both conflicted with my work schedule."

"According to Marjorie, he's head over heels for you." Mateo lifted his eyebrows. "You really didn't suspect?"

"No. I thought he was asking as a friend." Nina hadn't suspected his crush. She had thought they were in comfy friend territory. Tucker was quiet, not the least bit outgoing. He didn't even really talk to her that much. Now that she knew about his crush, she could imagine how hard it had been for him to ask her out. If that's what he'd been doing. He was a loner, for sure. Had she angered him by turning him down? While she wanted to see her attacker caught, she didn't want her attacker to be Tucker. Yet, now that she thought about it, she recalled catching him looking at her. She'd thought it was a coincidence, no big deal. But had there been malice behind that interest? Anger that she'd turned him down?

"What about the note he left?"

It had actually been a Bible verse combined with a note.

The fear of man bringeth a snare: But whoso putteth his trust in the LORD shall be safe.
Stay safe, Nina.

Mateo shrugged. "Maybe it was a backhanded threat. You know, the bit about a snare."

Could he be right? Or was Mateo just used to looking for the worst in people?

"If he wanted to encourage you, as he said, I don't get why he didn't just talk to you," Mateo said. "Why sneak around and put a note on my vehicle?"

"I don't know. I'm sure he saw I was with you. You are rather intimidating."

He frowned. "You find me intimidating?"

"The first time we met, yes." She shrugged. "You wanted

to interrogate my brother and would not take no for an answer."

"I wanted to *interview* your brother. I knew he was one of the good guys. There's a difference." He chuckled. "You were pretty formidable yourself. I recall you tried to have me removed from his hospital room."

"He was injured. He needed to rest."

"I was trying to wrap up a big case. I needed his testimony."

Her lips twitched. "You got it."

"And you stood by his bedside the whole time, making sure I didn't rile him up too much."

That was true. She had worked at the hospital back then, and while she hadn't been on duty, she had taken advantage of her hospital privileges by not leaving Seth's side for much of the time.

She was surprised and a bit flattered that Mateo seemed to remember that long-ago encounter as well as she did. She pushed away from the table and began to clear it. "I'll take care of the dishes. You mentioned you wanted to check your emails."

"If you're sure."

Nina nodded. She needed to keep busy. Her mind kept wandering back to Tucker and she found herself second-guessing every conversation they'd had.

The rumble of thunder rolled closer as the sky continued to darken. She could feel the storm moving in. Leaves trembled on the trees. Rain had begun sprinkling down but she was sure they were in for much worse. Pushing the curtain aside, she glanced out at the tree line. The gentle rain began spattering in large hard droplets against the windowpane. The wind picked up and the trees seemed to swirl against the sky. Forks of lightning split through the steely gray clouds. She let the curtain fall back in place.

It was unlikely her attacker was out in the woods, watching. Not with this weather coming in.

She hoped. The thought made her shudder.

"Are you cold?" Mateo was sitting at the table, reading his email from his phone so he could stay caught up on his work. Nina knew he'd had to touch base with the police chief, and had been given approval for concentrating on Nina's case for the time being. That included sequestering her away.

"A little." Though that wasn't why she'd shuddered, it wasn't a lie. The temperature had dropped now that the storm was moving in.

"I could start a fire," he offered.

"I'll be fine." She gave him a smile and began scrubbing the few dishes they had used. A feeling of restlessness settled into her bones. The cabin was so small and she was full of nervous energy.

She was trying to stay out of his way to let him get some work done. He was now jotting something in the notebook that had been in his briefcase. She wondered if it had to do with her case, or another. She wasn't naïve enough to think that hers was the only one he was working on right now.

Despite her curiosity, she didn't want to disturb him. Earlier, Officer Hughes had let them know she'd interviewed Nina's pastor and the church secretary. Neither had recognized any of the items in the binder. They had logged over a dozen photos and every one of them seemed to be a dead end.

Just like the photos on her camera.

She quashed down her disappointment.

The roar of thunder caused the cabin to vibrate. The rain

beat down and Nina could hear the wind howling through the trees.

Mateo flipped his notebook shut and moved away from the table. "The storm is really picking up. I didn't realize it was supposed to get so bad."

The lights flickered as thunder boomed again.

Mateo moved from the kitchen as Nina dropped onto the battered recliner.

The lights flickered and then went out completely, leaving the cabin gloomy but not completely dark. Though, with night falling, it would be dark soon enough.

"Mateo?"

"It's okay. It's just the storm." He pulled the curtain over the sink closed because Nina had accidentally left it open just a crack. For a moment, she thought it was strange there was a curtain over every window, even the smallest ones, but then remembered that the cabin was owned by a retired sheriff. He probably had the coverings for just this reason. To keep anyone from being able to see in. Was that paranoia? Or just good planning?

Maybe it was a bit of both.

Next, he went to the kitchen cupboard and pulled out a jar.

No, Nina realized, not a jar. A candle.

He found matches in the drawer.

His efficiency made it clear he'd scoped the place out and knew exactly where the items were that he was looking for. He placed the candle on the fireplace hearth. It was dim enough that Nina suspected it wouldn't draw attention through the window, but cast a lovely warm glow that took the edge off the gloom.

The relentless rumble of thunder made the cabin perpetually shudder.

Nina trembled and wrapped her arms around herself. Coco roused from her spot on the rug and trotted over to Nina.

"Is she afraid of storms?" Mateo asked.

"No." Nina scooped the dog off the floor and into her lap. "But she senses I'm not crazy about them."

He settled onto the futon. Though he was seated, Nina thought he still looked alert. She noticed his gun was holstered and easily within reach. She was sure he was right about the storm knocking out the electricity. Yet it was reassuring to know he was prepared should it turn out to be more.

He braced his elbows on his knees and leaned forward, studying her. "You're afraid of storms?"

She winced. "I used to be terrified, to be honest. We were in a terrible storm when I was younger, maybe five or six. My family was on the way home from an out-of-town wedding. Dad thought we could beat the storm, but it moved in faster than expected. Back then, we didn't have a cell phone, didn't carry around the internet in our pockets and purses to check the weather on a whim. We got caught in a deluge. He had to pull over because he couldn't see the road in front of him. The wind picked up. We could hear trees breaking and falling. I was sure we were going to be crushed. I was sitting in the very back of Mom's minivan with Ella. She held my hand and whispered over and over that everything was going to be okay. My brothers were in front of us, their noses pressed to the glass, trying to take in everything."

Mateo's lips quirked. "I don't know Eric and Seth well, but I can picture them doing that." Then he turned serious. "You and Ella were close?"

"She and Eric were twins, so I guess you could say they

had a special bond." Her memory flittered back in time. There were years when thinking about Ella would hurt so badly she felt as if her heart would break all over again at any simple memory. She was mostly past that now and could remember her sister with fondness. "But I was the baby of the family. She watched over me. I adored her and wanted to be just like her when I grew up."

"I'm sure she'd be proud of you now."

His words touched Nina's heart. "I hope so. It's because of her I decided to become a hospice nurse."

He nodded slowly. "I wondered why you'd chosen that path. You're so young. So vibrant. I hope I don't sound insensitive, because I admire what you do, but it seems like such a morose job for someone as young as you."

The fact that he had mentioned her age twice did not slip past Nina's notice. Was he bothered by her age? Or only surprised by it in relation to her chosen profession?

"You don't sound insensitive, but on that note, I don't find it morose." She often found it difficult to explain how she felt about her career. "Yes, there's a lot of sadness, but there's also a lot of hope. The hospice program I work for is Christian based. It's an honor to be with those who are slipping from this life to the next, knowing that Jesus is waiting for them there."

He leaned back, his expression unreadable.

"You don't agree?"

Coco whimpered and slipped off her lap. She trotted over to Mateo.

Nina wondered what that was about. Coco seemed to be in tune with people's emotions. Nina believed God gave dogs the gift of feeling others' emotions in a way that humans couldn't. She had no proof of this, and sure, she could be wrong, but she'd seen enough service dogs in action to think that something special was happening here.

He cleared his throat. "You make it sound so simple. I think death is a lot more complicated than that."

Complicated wasn't a surprise. Mateo seemed like a complicated man.

"It's only complicated to the people left behind," Nina murmured. "I know you said you have some family around. You didn't mention a wife. Is there anyone special?"

His eyes shot to hers.

She felt her cheeks redden because she knew it was a nosy question. "I'm just wondering if I'm keeping you from someone."

He paused a few beats. "No, there's no one."

Coco let out a soft whimper and laid her head on his knee. He smiled faintly at her and gave her shoulders a vigorous rubbing.

Nina watched the scene with a mixture of interest and concern. She'd seen Coco do the same thing countless times before. What kind of troubling emotion had Coco sensed emanating from Mateo? Sadness? Anxiety?

She wanted to ask but she'd already been a bit too curious. Instead, she let Coco do her thing. Mateo continued to pet her and Nina was sure she could see some of the tension melt from his shoulders. Coco sighed as if relieved.

When he glanced at Nina again, he gave her a faint smile.

"Sorry, I didn't mean to pry," she said. "I just want you to know how grateful I am that you're here with me." Worried how that would sound, she hurried on. "When I sneaked out of the house, I had every intention of taking off on my own. I wasn't looking forward to it. Honestly, I was scared to death, even though I felt it was the right thing to do to keep my family safe. I'm glad I'm not alone."

"It's no problem." Mateo leaned back. Coco wriggled around beside him, making herself comfortable while staying close. "Just doing my job."

Right. His job.

Of course, she knew that, but she didn't like the reminder. An unreasonable part of her wanted him to be there because he *wanted* to be. But he was right. He was guarding her because it was his job. Nothing more, nothing less.

She couldn't help but wonder, though, was he trying to convince her of that? Or himself?

Mateo wished the lights would come back on. He wanted the storm to stop. This conversation with Nina had started to feel far too personal.

He did not do personal.

He didn't want to talk about himself. Nor did he want to bring up the case right now. Nina was already wound tight enough. Besides, at this juncture, there was nothing new to discuss, so best to let it rest and not bring it up at all.

Conversely, while he would like to get to know Nina better, he knew asking her about herself was a bad idea. He already knew enough to do his job. No need to be nosy and try to find out more. Because if he did, he would have to admit to himself that he was only asking because he was curious.

He needed to stay professional.

Mind whirling, he tried to think of something neutral to talk about.

"Other than Mrs. Wallace, the people at the Senior Center really seem to like Coco." He stroked the dog's head. She leaned into him. Maybe he should get a dog. No. He'd thought about that before. As much as he'd like to, he wasn't home enough.

Nina's eyes sparkled. "Yes, most people do."

"I've met K-9 dogs. Search-and-rescue and bomb-sniffing dogs. But I've never seen a therapy dog at work before. What exactly does she do?"

Nina arched an eyebrow and pointed at him.

He tried not to notice how pretty she looked in the flickering of the candlelight. Instead, he glanced down at the dog resting beside him, her head on his lap.

"She takes naps on people?"

She chuckled. "Not exactly. I believe she senses when people are upset. I mean we sense when others are upset, but I think dogs feel it on a deeper level. When she senses heavy emotions in people she…" Nina paused, as if searching for the right words. "Well, I guess she loves on them and usually that helps bring a sense of calm."

It took him a moment to wrap his head around what Nina was saying. She had clearly given him a pointed look.

"Wait." He jerked his hand back as he looked at the dog soaking up his attention. She lifted her head and blinked at him, awakened by his sudden movement. Here he'd thought he was doing the little rascal a favor by petting her. Was it the other way around? He narrowed his eyes at the cocker spaniel and she stared back at him. Those deep brown puppy-dog eyes seemed filled with emotion. "Are you saying she's sensing something…from me?"

"That's what she does. Yes."

Mateo glanced from Nina to Coco then back at Nina. "You think she's sensing heavy emotions from me? And what, using her special puppy powers to calm me?"

Nina laughed lightly. It was a refreshing sound, even if her laughter was over his question.

"Don't sound so horrified by that. There's nothing wrong with being stressed and needing a little calming with her—"

she made air quotes with her fingers "—'special puppy power.' I don't know anyone whose emotions are even keel all the time."

Here he thought he'd hidden his emotions so well.

He glanced at the dog again, feeling as if Nina's furry friend had betrayed him. He was unreasonably annoyed by that.

"I can tell you're carrying something heavy." Nina's words were gentle. "Coco isn't the only one who can sense that. Want to talk about it?"

Suddenly it seemed like the shack was closing in on him. No one had asked him that in ages. The last person had been Mara, his sister. Yes, he'd had a few friends who had tried to get him to open up, but he'd always shut them down. It was part of the reason he'd left Bozeman, where his parents and sister resided. The town where his family had perished.

He'd moved to Mulberry Creek for a fresh start. To get away from sympathetic glances and prying questions. Only, instead of the fresh start he'd hoped for, he felt unfilled and alone. So very alone.

He did not want to talk about Jolene and his boys. Not ever.

Only now, somehow with Nina, he felt like he did.

But he couldn't. He and Nina didn't have that kind of relationship. They had *no* relationship at all, really. Other than that she was in danger and it was his job to protect her.

Right. Keep reminding yourself of that, buddy. Because you seem awfully close to forgetting.

Yet he knew, with almost complete assurance, that if anyone would understand, it would be her. He could not cross that line, though. It would be too easy to slide down that slippery slope.

He needed to keep things professional.

"Did something happen with your job? Did a case go sideways?" Nina asked.

It was a good guess. He'd had his share of tough cases. Seen his share of rough, unpleasant things. But nothing compared to what he'd gone through in his personal life.

"No. Not my job." Why had he admitted that?

"Something personal then."

Nina's tone was soft and the look she gave him made his insides stir, made his cold hardened heart beat a little faster. She was looking at him like she cared. But what did that mean? Did she care the same way she would with any other person Coco had taken notice of? Or did she care about him in the same way he was coming to care about her?

It wasn't as if he could ask.

Yet maybe he *could* open up to her and tell her about Jolene and the boys. He found himself wanting to. Nina was so open and honest. He felt as if she would listen and try to understand what he'd gone through and how it still affected him.

But no, he couldn't.

The thought terrified him. Ridiculous that the big, tough detective was afraid of opening up to someone. Besides, the timing was all wrong.

He was working a case right now. Nina's case.

"I'm sorry." Nina winced. "I don't mean to pry. Just because I told you about Ella, that doesn't mean that you have to share anything with me. I thought maybe you wanted to talk, but, clearly, I was wrong."

Actually, she was right. He wanted desperately to tell her so. It had been so long since he'd confided in someone. Now it seemed impossible to get the words out. Like they were all locked up inside and he'd lost the key.

Coco whimpered and nudged his hand. He was tempted to yank it away, but it was too late. Nina had seen. A slight crease rested between her brows but she didn't say anything. He glanced down at the dog, giving her an accusatory look. Coco's head was tilted to the side as she gazed up at him. It was silly, impossible, he was sure, but he was certain the dog was looking at him with concern.

Could she sense his emotions? That seemed ludicrous. And yet…

He couldn't deny that in this moment his emotions did seem to be a swirling mixed-up jumble.

He gently slid Coco's head from his lap. She let out a sound of disappointment before she trotted over to Nina.

"Mateo?"

"I should do a perimeter check."

"It's still raining." She frowned. "I really don't think anyone is out there."

"I won't melt." He shrugged. "And we can't be too careful."

He strode toward the door and out into the wet evening though he didn't believe for one second there was anyone out there. Leaning against the side of the cabin, barely sheltered under the eve, he pulled in a deep breath. Then exhaled slowly. He needed to find this attacker, needed to put him behind bars.

Then he needed to send Nina and her pesky pooch back to her parents' ranch. *Then* he could get back to status quo.

Because having them both here…was just causing too much chaos for his battered heart.

EIGHT

The next morning the sky was heavy with clouds, leaving Mateo wondering if they were in for more bad weather. Much to his relief, the electricity had been restored sometime in the middle of the night. It was reassuring to know that while they were sequestered, they weren't so far from civilization that they were forgotten by the rest of the world.

He hadn't slept well the night before. The storm, his strained conversation with Nina, and the questioning of Tucker were all on his mind. They hadn't had enough reason to hold the guy, so he'd been released. Mateo didn't know what to make of the questioning. It bothered him that Tucker had lied. He should've known better. But did that make him guilty? No. However, Mateo wasn't convinced of his innocence, either. He was going to stay neutral on the matter until they had more facts.

He'd stayed outside far too long last night in the rain. Nina had gone upstairs before he'd come back in. She'd gotten the hint he hadn't wanted to talk anymore.

He heard the loft door open, followed by her soft footsteps on the staircase.

"Good morning." She wore a tentative smile as she entered the kitchen. "What do we have planned for today? Is visiting Golden Acres still on the agenda?"

Whether Tucker was guilty or not, there was no denying they still needed more evidence. That evidence would either prove his guilt or innocence.

"It is." Mateo lifted his cup and took a sip. He was grateful that Nina didn't mention last night. He felt a bit foolish now for running out into the rain, but at the time he'd just needed to get away. "There's plenty of coffee left if you'd like to help yourself."

Coco did a wiggly little dance at the door.

"Looks like we need to take care of business first. We'll be right back." She grabbed the leash she'd hung on a coat hook. After clipping it to Coco's collar and sliding her shoes on, they went outside. Mateo stood and watched through the window. He was sure they were safe outside, but there were no guarantees. He wasn't going to take any chances of Nina disappearing on him. She walked Coco to the edge of the forest and let her do her thing. Then Coco trotted toward the door and they came back inside.

Nina quickly filled the dog's food and water dishes then took a seat across from him. He had a cup of coffee waiting for her.

While he was grateful she hadn't brought it up, he wondered if he should apologize for last night. He didn't really want to talk about it. Definitely didn't want to draw attention to his cantankerous behavior, but he was afraid guilt would get the better of him. Before he could think it over too long, his phone rang.

He glanced at it and then shot Nina a hopeful look before answering. "Hey, Jimmy. Tell me you have something for me."

"I do. I decided this place could use a good organizing. I've been cleaning up since you left. At least, when there hasn't been anyone in the store."

"Uh-huh," Mateo said. "And?"

"I found the guy's name." Jimmy sounded pleased with himself. "Have his number, too. You still want the info?"

"You know I do."

"I'll text to it to you in a minute. Just thought I'd mention that I remembered something else. This guy, name's Lyle Weintzel, by the way, said his wife was in a nursing home and the cost was eating up his savings. Said he'd maybe stop by with some other items for me to look at, but he never did."

"A nursing home?" Mateo's interest was piqued. "Did he happen to say which one?"

"Boy, I'm not sure."

"Any chance it was Golden Acres?" Mateo knew he risked the power of suggestion, but threw it out there anyway.

"You know…" Jimmy paused, as if thinking it over. "I think he did say that. Said it was a nice place and he was happy with the care she was receiving."

"Thanks, Jimmy."

"Sure thing. I hope this pans out for you. I'll send the information now."

They said a quick goodbye and then Mateo's phone pinged with the text.

It was the man's name along with his phone number.

"Do you have a lead?" Nina asked.

"Sure do. Jimmy came through for me. The man with the stamps? His name is Lyle Weintzel. Do you know him?"

Her brow furrowed. "I don't think so. Should I?"

He shrugged. "Probably not. But Lyle's wife is in a nursing home."

"Golden Acres?"

"Jimmy thinks so. I get that it's a big place, so you're

not going to know everyone. But if his wife really is there, that could be a connection."

"Are you going to call him?"

"Since this is our only lead so far, and it's shaky at best, I don't want to give him the chance to blow me off." Mateo tapped on his phone, looking up the man's address. "Looks like he lives on Birch Street, right near the downtown area."

"We're going to go see him?"

"Yes. I want to speak with him in person."

Nina finished off her coffee. "Let's go."

He admired her gumption and they left without delay.

Lyle's place was easy enough to find. The street was lined with older homes. His appeared to be meticulously well-kept. Colorful flowers bloomed in the flower bed that lined the front porch.

A Ford truck, several decades old but devoid of rust, sat in the driveway.

Mateo parked at the curb. He glanced around. The street was quiet with only a few people out in their yards. It was the middle of the workday, so he wasn't surprised. A few vehicles rolled past but none of them caused him any concern.

"Let's go see if he's home." Mateo grabbed the binder. "We're due for a real break in this case."

They quickly strode up the sidewalk. Mateo knocked firmly on the door. When no one answered, he knocked again.

"Hold yer horses!"

"At least he's home," Nina murmured.

The door was tugged open and a frail-looking elderly gentleman frowned at them. "I wasn't expecting company."

"I'm sorry, sir," Mateo began, "but if I could just have a few minutes of your time?"

The man's bushy white eyebrows narrowed in suspicion. "Why?"

"I was told you own a rather unique stamp collection."

The man's eyes lit with interest. "That so? You in the market to buy them?"

The way the man spoke, it sounded as if he was still in possession of them.

Mateo sidestepped the question. "Do you still have them?"

Was it possible he didn't know they were missing? Or had Jimmy been mistaken about the items?

"I do." The man looked at Nina. "You look familiar. Do I know you?"

"I'm not sure." She gave him an endearing smile. "I heard your wife is at Golden Acres. I volunteer there on occasion."

He snapped his fingers. "That's right. You're the dog lady!"

"Uh, yes."

He peered over her shoulder. "Well, where is she?"

"In the car," Nina said. "We left the windows open a crack for fresh air. And it's not too warm out today."

After last night's storm, it was downright chilly.

"Awww, go get her, would ya?"

"I'll do it." Mateo trotted down the steps. He heard Lyle pick up the conversation.

"I've seen that dog around but haven't had the chance to greet her personally," he said.

"You like dogs?" Nina asked.

"Who doesn't?"

Mateo returned with Coco on her leash.

Lyle winced when his back cracked and popped, but that didn't stop him from bending over to pet the pooch.

"What a good lil' girl you are," he said.

Mateo's eyes met Nina's. She flashed him a grin. Seemed

everyone adored Coco. Mateo had to admit, the dog was hard not to like, even if she was a fluffy little traitor.

"All right," Lyle said as he creakily straightened again, "you wanted to see my stamps?"

"I do."

"Come on in." Lyle held the door open and stood back to allow them entrance.

Mateo was immediately struck by how clean the house was. Everything seemed to be in its place. There was no clutter, no stacks or piles of anything. The furniture and carpet were dated and worn, but appeared to have been treated with love. The scent of lemon furniture polish clung to the air.

"You have a very nice home," Nina said.

"Thank you." Lyle glanced around the room as if trying to see it through Nina's eyes. "The missus was a fussy housekeeper. I know it's silly, but I don't want to disappoint her by letting this place go to the dumps."

"It's not silly," Nina assured him. "It's very sweet."

"You two have a seat," Lyle ordered. "I'll go fetch the collection."

Mateo and Nina did as instructed, Coca resting near Nina's feet.

She leaned closer to Mateo and whispered, "I thought his stamps were in the lockbox? How can he still have them?"

"Either he has a similar set and Jimmy was mistaken," Mateo said, "or they aren't here after all."

A few moments later, they had their answer.

Lyle stomped into the living room. He rubbed a hand over his face. "They're gone. My stamps are gone. So's my cash. Nearly a thousand dollars of emergency money. It's gone."

Mateo rose to his feet. "Have you let anyone, other than us, into your house recently?"

Lyle frowned. "Just family. Don't get much company other than my kids and grandkids."

"Have you noticed any sign of forced entry?"

"No." His brow wrinkled in thought. "Can't say that I have."

"Do you lock your doors?"

"Yes. Of course." He hefted an aggrieved sigh. "Mostly."

Mostly. Mateo was afraid of that.

"Sometimes I forget," he admitted.

"When is the last time you remember seeing your collection?"

Lyle shot him a suspicious look. "Why all the questions?"

Mateo took out his badge and held it for Lyle to inspect. "I'm with the Mulberry Creek Police Department. I have reason to suspect your collection was stolen. When you said it was here, I was hoping I was wrong and we could just be on our way."

"Stolen." Lyle spat the word. "Right out of my house?"

"Do you recall when you saw them last?" Mateo pressed. "It's important. Then I'll fill you in on what we know."

"Pretty sure the last time I saw them was when I brought them to the pawn shop guy. Jerry, I think. Must've been a few months ago, at least."

"Jimmy," Mateo lightly corrected.

"Jimmy." Lyle slapped his thigh. "That's it. Did he take my stamps?"

"No," Mateo assured him.

"I think I need to sit." Lyle collapsed into the threadbare recliner.

Coco made a sound of commiseration then trotted over to him. She rested her head against Lyle's knee. Lyle leaned forward and scooped the small dog up, placing her in his lap. She didn't protest, simply pressed her head against his chest. She sat patiently as he methodically stroked her fur.

Nina's heart went out to the elderly gentleman. Mateo had handled the situation as gently as could be expected. Lyle looked utterly flabbergasted as he realized that his home had been violated. He looked around, as if inspecting everything with a newly critical eye.

Mateo gave him the binder and when Lyle flipped to the page with the photo of his stamps, his expression hardened. "That's them. That's them right there."

Nina hadn't really doubted, but it was good to have confirmation.

Lyle stroked Coco mindlessly, methodically, as he took a big breath. "It's hard to believe someone was in my home and I didn't even notice."

"Did you talk about your collection at the nursing home?" Mateo asked.

"My wife is very proud of my stamps. They've been in my family a long time. It's come up a time or two."

"Where did you keep them?" Mateo asked.

"In a shoebox under my bed," Lyle said. "Same place they've been for decades."

Nina and Mateo shared a look. She was wondering if perhaps his wife had unwittingly shared Lyle's secret.

It became clear quickly that while the stamps were Lyle's, he had no idea who could have taken them.

Mateo and Nina stood.

Cocoa jumped off Lyle's lap.

He stood as well.

"If you think of anything, anyone suspicious, or remember any incident that happened here that didn't seem important at the time, give me a call. Even if it's something small." Mateo handed him a card.

They left with a promise from Mateo that Lyle's collection would be returned to him as soon as possible.

"Well, that was a bummer," Nina said as they slid into Mateo's Tahoe. "I feel bad for the guy. His stamps were stolen and he didn't even realize it."

"At least they were recovered." Mateo winced. "Unlike the money."

They were only halfway down the block when Mateo's phone rang. He glanced at the screen. "It's Lyle."

Nina wondered if they'd forgotten something, but she was certain that other than the binder and Coco, they hadn't taken anything in.

He answered, telling Lyle he was on speakerphone because he was driving.

"I just thought of something," Lyle said.

"Yeah, what's that?"

Mateo shot a quick look at Nina.

"You let me look through that binder that you have. I was in a rush to get to the page with my stamps, but something has been needling at me since you left." Lyle paused then huffed out a breath. "Now, I can't be certain, mind you, because I was flipping through the pages so fast, but I'm pretty sure I recall seeing that nice ruby brooch before."

Nina's heart skittered.

Mateo's voice remained calm, but Nina noticed how his hands tightened on the steering wheel. "Do you recall where?"

"Sure do. A nice lady by the name of Beatrice Walker."

Nina knew that name.

Lyle continued. "Her husband's a resident of Golden Acres. I've seen her around with him. He's in a wheelchair but she takes him out into the courtyard every chance she gets. She's always dressed real fancy. I think they probably come from money. I guess it's possible it's not the same brooch. But it sure does look a lot like it."

"Thank you, Lyle," Mateo said. "That's very helpful."

"You think so?" He sounded hopeful. "You think it might help catch this guy?"

"If your suspicion pans out, it sure might," Mateo said. "Thank you for telling me. I'll be in touch."

Mateo disconnected and turned to Nina.

She arched a brow. "Next stop, Beatrice Walker's house?"

He nodded. "You know it."

It didn't take long to track down Beatrice's address and drive to the other side of town. Unlike Lyle's home, hers was in a fancy neighborhood. The brick two-story home was picture-perfect. No chipped or peeling paint in sight.

On a hunch that Beatrice would not approve of Coco in her immaculate home, they left her in the car. The windows were open far enough to ensure the cool breeze would keep her comfortable.

Nina noticed everything about the home looked pristine. She thought Lyle was right. This family had money.

Mateo rang the bell. She could hear the sound reverberating through the house. It took only a few moments before a lovely elderly woman opened the door. Her hair was as white as a cotton ball, her sparkling blue eyes as bright as a sapphire. Her face was perfectly made up, as if she were on her way out the door.

"Mrs. Walker?" Mateo asked.

"Yes? Can I help you?"

Mateo held out his badge. "I do hope so. Could I ask for a few minutes of your time?"

She blinked at him in confusion then worry. "Are my children all right?"

Nina had to guess her children were middle-aged, but mothers never stopped being mothers.

"We're here about a ruby brooch."

That statement got them through the door.

Beatrice led them to the kitchen where she offered them coffee. They both declined and then, while seated at the kitchen table, Mateo got down to business. He explained what they had discovered, how a gentleman had recalled seeing her wear the brooch at Golden Acres, and why they were there now.

He slid the binder toward her, opened to the page with the item in question.

Beatrice stared at them in disbelief. "I thought I lost that brooch. I've looked high and low for it. I finally assumed that it must've fallen off. The clasp was wobbly at one time, but I'd had it fixed. It belonged to my mother."

Nina gritted her teeth at the confirmation. What kind of rotten person stole from the elderly?

"You're *sure* it's your brooch?" Mateo asked.

"Very sure." Beatrice stood and hurried out of the room. In a matter of minutes, she was back, holding a picture frame. She held it out for Mateo and Nina to view. "My husband and me."

Nina thought it looked like the sort of picture taken for a church directory. It was a close-up and the brooch affixed to Beatrice's emerald-green blazer was clearly the same brooch that was in the binder. The ruby was massive and the gold enclosing it was ornate.

They went through the same round of questions with Beatrice as they had with Lyle. She perused the binder, looking at every photo carefully, but none of the items, other than her brooch, was familiar to her.

From her vantage point Nina caught sight of the diamond-crusted crucifix again as Beatrice turned the pages. It niggled at her. She was sure she'd seen it. But where? It couldn't have been recently or she wouldn't be having such a terrible time trying to remember. Had it belonged to a resident at Golden Acres? No. Residents of the nursing home weren't allowed to keep anything valuable with them. The rooms weren't private like rooms in an assisted living facility. The residents' doors were not locked in case they needed immediate care, which would've left valuables vulnerable.

A visitor then?

She was so frustrated with herself. She wished she could remember. Or maybe she was completely wrong. Maybe she had only seen something similar at one time.

They wrapped up their visit after Beatrice obtained a promise from Mateo that the brooch would be returned to her.

Because Golden Acres seemed to be the common link, they headed there next.

Mateo let Nina sign them in then she introduced him to the director of the nursing home. She gave her permission for him to question the residents as long as they were willing.

Nina suspected many would be willing. Most of the residents were hungry for company. Nina didn't know everyone at Golden Acres, but she'd grown close to a few residents. Primarily those who came to visit Coco in the large comfortable room Nina had dubbed the parlor. That was their first stop.

A small group of women was seated around a table, playing a card game.

"Hi, ladies." Nina edged up to the table. "How is the game going?"

Mildred, a woman Nina had known from the Senior Center before she'd become a resident at Golden Acres, greeted her warmly.

"What are you up to today?" Mildred asked the question as she gave Mateo a thorough once-over. "And who do you have with you?"

"This is a friend of mine. His name is Mateo." Nina introduced him to the group, naming the women as she went around the table.

"A friend." Mildred's eyes lit up. She grinned conspiratorially at Nina. "A very handsome friend, too."

Nina flashed Mateo a look that was half apology, half amusement. "Mildred, he's not that kind of friend. Not the sort you're implying. He's just a…pal. A buddy."

"Mmm-hmm," the woman hummed. "I've heard that line before. It's almost always nonsense."

Nina laughed. "I assure you, this time it's the truth."

"We'll see." Mildred sounded very sure of herself. "Time will tell. I have a knack for sensing these things."

"I'm here for a reason…" Nina pushed ahead.

"To let me visit with that lovely pup of yours?" Wilma asked. The woman adored Coco and Nina knew she would keep her all to herself if she could. She held out her hand from the other side of the table, reaching for Coco's leash. "May I?"

"Of course." Nina led Coco around the table and handed the leash off to Wilma. The woman smiled down at Coco, who began nuzzling her knee.

"What really brings you by?" Mildred asked, circling the conversation back around.

Nina dove into the issue at hand, explaining everything in detail for what felt like the thousandth time.

"How exciting," Mildred declared. "I love a good mystery. Let's take a look at that binder of yours."

Nina wasn't expecting much. She certainly wasn't expecting Mildred to recognize the pendant that took up the first page. It was the piece that had seemed so familiar to Nina, but that she couldn't place. "Why, this belonged to Gloria Hanson."

Yes!

The moment Mildred said the name, everything clicked. She had met Gloria at the Senior Center. Now that her memory had been jostled, Nina could clearly envision the woman wearing the pendant.

"She had a nasty fall," Mildred continued. "Why someone her age was trying to go into the cellar is beyond me. I know my limitations and I would never do such a thing."

"That's right," Nina murmured, remembering now.

Mildred flipped the page again. "Oh! This one here! This belongs to Beatrice Walker. I'm sure of it. I know it went missing a few months ago. She thought she'd lost it."

"Yes, it's hers." Mateo kept his tone conversational but Nina knew he was absorbing every word. "We've spoken with her already. She'll be reunited with her brooch soon."

Mildred nodded her approval. Her eyes widened when she spotted the Rolex. "Well, I do believe this belongs to Chester Crenshaw. It was a gift from his eldest son and he was terribly proud of it. Always telling anyone who would listen that his son was quite the moneymaker. Showed it off every chance he got." Mildred glanced at Nina. "Do you remember him, dear?"

Chester Crenshaw.

"Yes. I knew him from the Senior Center, though not well." She locked eyes with Mateo as a shiver shimmied down her spine. She tried to silently convey that she had so much more to tell him about Chester Crenshaw, that it wasn't something she wanted to share in front of this group of women. He gave her an almost-imperceptible nod to let her know he understood.

Mildred continued to page through the binder as the ladies sitting with her craned their heads to view it, too. When she got to the end, she flipped it closed.

"That's all. I only recognize those three items." She glanced around the table at her group of friends. "I assume none of you recognized anything or you would have piped up."

"Not a thing," Hazel said.

"Only Beatrice's brooch," Wilma conceded.

That made sense as Nina knew the other two women had been residents of Golden Acres for quite some time. Nina didn't ever remember them visiting the Senior Center, which was where Mildred recognized both the pendant and the Rolex from.

Was the Senior Center the common link? They had begun to think it was the nursing home after identifying the owners of the stamps and brooch.

A thought occurred to her.

"Mildred, do you know if either Gloria Hanson or Chester Crenshaw had a spouse here? A reason to visit?"

"Not that I'm aware of." Mildred rubbed her temple as if trying to coax her memories loose. "But I could be wrong. I do believe that Gloria had a good friend here. I think I remember her mentioning that during one of our Thursday knitting meetings held at the Senior Center. Though, for the life of me, I can't think of who. She's been gone nearly a year now, you know. I can't seem to remember many details that far back." The woman looked perturbed over her memory loss.

Mateo placed a hand on her shoulder. "It's quite all right. You've been very helpful."

Mildred beamed at him. "Have I? It's been the longest time since I've felt useful."

"You have," he assured her.

Nina frowned as she glanced around. "Wilma, where's Coco?"

Wilma looked startled. She looked down at her hand, which was no longer holding the leash, as if surprised by the question. "Oh, dear. I must've let go of her."

Nina spun around, her eyes darting across the room. "It's not like her to wander off."

Mateo reached over and grabbed the binder off the table. "Thank you all so much for your help. It was nice meeting you, but we have a dog to find."

Nina waved a hurried goodbye as she hustled out of the parlor.

"Coco is welcomed here," Nina said, "but that was with the agreement that she would be kept under control at all times. While I'm sure she's not wreaking havoc, she certainly isn't supposed to be wandering about freely."

Nina's shoes slapped against the linoleum floor as Mateo kept pace with her. She glanced into each room they passed by.

"Does she have a favorite friend here? Someone she might wander off to see?" he asked.

Just then, Nina spotted a furry fanny with a stubby little tail that wiggled as if in overdrive. A purple leash trailed behind.

"Coco." Nina's voice was firm, commanding, as she hustled down the hallway to her dog. The spaniel's back end was sticking out of the corridor and when they rounded it, they realized she was chomping on something.

"What do you have?" Nina demanded.

But Coco had swallowed whatever she'd been munching on, leaving no trace of evidence. Nina whirled, looking up and down the hallway. No one was in sight. Then she grabbed the dog's leash.

"Do you think she got into something she shouldn't have?" Mateo asked.

"I think someone probably gave her a treat without getting permission," Nina admitted. "It happens. Most people ask, but some just take the liberty of tossing her a snack." She winced. "I'm so embarrassed. Usually, she's better behaved than this. She hasn't been a therapy dog for long, but I thought we had the rules down."

She noticed the clock on the wall. "It's getting close to dinnertime. Do you want to question anyone else? We don't have much time before everyone begins filing into the dining room."

"Not today," Mateo said. "I have a feeling there's something you want to share with me."

Nina's eyes flitted up and down the hallway as her thoughts swirled back around to Chester Crenshaw. "Yes."

A chill cascaded down her spine.

Both Chester and Gloria were tied to the Senior Center and both had perished in falls, though the falls were nearly a year apart. Both had also had items stolen from them. Her thoughts fluttered to Tucker. He'd been volunteering at the center at least that long. Could he be the attacker after all?

"We need to talk, but not here." Nina kept her voice low.

She didn't think anyone was within hearing distance though she wasn't going to take that chance.

Coco dropped to her haunches and scratched at her neck with her back foot, causing her nametag to jingle. It sounded ridiculously loud to Nina's ears. She scooped Coco up and headed for the door. Since her hands were full, Mateo signed them out.

She appreciated that he waited until they were a distance from the lot before questioning her.

"Okay. What do you know?" He gave her an expectant look as they headed out of town.

"I knew Chester Crenshaw. Not just from the Senior Center. What Mildred didn't mention was that he also died from an accidental fall."

"'Accidental.'" Mateo arched a brow. "Go on."

"He slipped in his kitchen. Hit his head on the tile floor. Never regained consciousness." Nina pulled in a breath. "His family wanted him to pass in familiar surroundings. They'd brought him home from the hospital. I was his hospice nurse."

"So we have two deaths. Both of them falls, yet because they were elderly, I assume the falls weren't looked into."

"Correct. But there's more."

He looked at her expectantly.

"When I'm working with a patient, I do my best to give the family privacy. Yet sometimes it's impossible not to overhear conversations." Nina paused briefly. "Mateo, his two sons were arguing. Quite loudly. One son accused the other of stealing a coffee can full of money. He mentioned that since their dad had lived through the Great Depression, he didn't trust banks and his life savings was stored inside the house. In the kitchen cabinet. In a coffee can. He didn't say how much, but I got the impression it was quite substantial. He also mentioned a missing watch. I assume now he meant the Rolex."

"How long ago was this?"

"I haven't been with hospice long." Nina ran a hand through her hair as she thought about it. "I'd say this happened a month ago, at the most. Our agency keeps record of everything, of course, so they could confirm the exact date."

Mateo didn't say anything for several long moments.

When he finally spoke, he looked grim. "We don't have enough information to open a full-blown investigation into these deaths. I do agree, given the circumstances, they seem suspicious. I'll try to do some digging. One thing that has become obvious, whether it's the Senior Center, the nursing home, or your work in hospice—all of which are tied to the stolen goods, and therefore the attacker—*you* seem to be the common link."

They had known from the start that there had to be more to this case than a man burying trinkets in the park. Even if the items had been stolen, which they obviously had been, and worth a great deal of money. But what if these deaths were not accidental? Two falls resulting in the passing of at least two of the people who'd been robbed. Could they be dealing with a murderer?

A sense of dread cascaded over her.

"That's not our only problem." Mateo's voice was terse and Nina realized he had spotted something in the rear-view mirror.

She whirled around in her seat to check out the road behind them. Her heart nearly exploded from her chest. A vehicle was behind them, gaining fast. That in itself wasn't what had her heart racing.

That she could blame on the gun sticking out the window, pointing right at them.

NINE

How had they been followed? Had someone put a tracking device on Mateo's Tahoe? The car behind them seemed to have come from nowhere. Nina dug her phone out of her purse, intending to call 911.

Boom.

The sound of gunshot split the air. Nina let out a shriek of surprise.

The SUV skidded as a tire blew. It fishtailed and Nina knew they were going to roll an instant before the vehicle actually did. She dropped her phone, the call unfinished.

"Hold on!" Mateo's voice was a growl.

The impact was juddering, every bone in her body felt as if it was being slammed around. She clenched her teeth in an effort to keep from crying out. Everything blended together as Nina's seat belt held her, almost painfully, in place. The airbags deployed. The vehicle slammed onto the roof, then back again, once…twice…she couldn't keep track.

Coco yipped from the back seat and Nina was grateful for the doggy car seat her niece and nephew had giggled over.

It felt as though they'd hit a brick wall when they came to a jarring stop.

Nina slowly opened her eyes. The airbag that had held

her in place was already deflating. She twisted around to see Mateo slumped against the driver's door. His deployed airbag was also shrinking by the second. The window was cracked and a large tree was on the other side.

That, she realized, was what had stopped them in place. At least they had landed right-side up.

"Mateo." Her voice was shaky. Pain ricocheted through her body but she didn't think anything was broken. Her heart skittered in her chest when Mateo didn't move. "Mateo!"

It was then that she saw the blood trickling down the window, pooling from a gash she could not see.

Coco whimpered from the back. She twisted around to find the dog securely strapped in place, staring at her. Frightened but seemingly unharmed.

In an instant, she remembered what had caused the crash. Someone had been pursuing them. They'd been chased then shot at. The tire had exploded.

Right.

Was that person still out there?

Most likely.

Swiveling her head, she scoped out their immediate surroundings for danger.

Mateo still hadn't moved. She saw the spider-webbing of glass throughout the window and suspected he'd hit his head. Hard. Probably when the SUV had slammed against the tree.

She needed to tend to Mateo, though nothing in her ever-present fanny pack would be a cure all for this dire situation. Then she needed to get him mobile so they could get out of here.

With great effort, she pushed the door wide. She shoved the airbag out of the way. They couldn't just sit there. It was too dangerous. She needed to formulate a plan. There didn't seem to be a part of her body that wasn't aching as she wiggled her way out the door. She nearly fell, still dizzy and disoriented from the crash, as she slid gracelessly from the vehicle.

And came face-to-face with a masked man.

She let out a yip of terror. Coco let out a commiserating yip of her own.

"Finally caught up to you."

"Who are you?" Nina demanded.

"Not for you to know."

She could see his eyes through the mask, but not much else. They were brown. Not as dark as Mateo's. But colder. So much colder.

What color eyes did Tucker have? Had she ever paid close enough attention? She couldn't remember. This man was the same size, but his voice was chilling.

"Looks like he smashed his head hard. Is he dead?" He motioned with his gun. From this vantage point, Mateo looked ghastly pale against the blood-streaked window. He was unmoving. "You're a nurse. Figure it out."

Her heart was hammering but she tried to ignore the gun pointed at her head. Leaning inside, she reached across her seat and pressed two fingers to Mateo's carotid artery. The pulse beating under her fingertips brought a wrenching sob to her lips.

The man mistook her sob of gratitude for one of despair.

"One down, one to go. Grab his gun."

She was *not* about to correct his misassumption.

"His gun," the man growled.

She moved without delay this time. If Mateo flinched, or moaned, made any sign of life at all, she suspected this man would shoot him point-blank. With shaking hands, she slid Mateo's gun from his holster.

Don't move, Mateo. Don't make a sound. Let him believe that you're dead.

His chest rose and fell, almost peacefully, and she prayed this man would not notice.

"Put the gun where I can see it."

The weapon felt foreign in Nina's hand. She came from a family of avid hunters, even her mother was good with a gun. But not Nina. She'd never had a desire to learn the skill. While she didn't have a problem with others hunting, she couldn't stomach the thought of doing so herself. She'd never learned to shoot.

This guy didn't have to tell her not to try anything with the gun because she didn't know how anyway. In that moment, she felt so utterly helpless. So alone.

But no, she wasn't alone.

God, please protect us. Watch over Mateo. I don't see a way out of this, but I know You can make a way where there is no way.

She turned, holding the gun gingerly, taking no chances he would see her as a threat.

"Toss it."

Nina did as she was told. The gun flew through the air and landed in the brush.

"Where are your phones?"

"I'll get them." Nina tugged Mateo's phone from where it was clipped to the dashboard. She fumbled with the airbag as she dug around for her phone on the floor.

Nina held them out to him. She longed to finish the call she hadn't been able to send, but couldn't. Not with this man watching her every move.

"Drop them."

She followed his command and he stomped on each, shattering the screens.

"Now toss them."

She picked them up and whipped them into the woods, realizing he didn't want his fingerprints on anything. Mateo's cell disappeared as his gun had, but her phone hit a tree and bounced back to the ground.

"Good enough," he snarled. "Now let's move."

The order seemed to reverberate through her.

"Okay." She took a step toward him. More importantly, she took a step *away* from Mateo. It was the only thing she could think of to do that would protect him. She had to get this man away from him before Mateo awoke. *If* he awoke. A frisson of misery coursed through her. It was killing her that she couldn't tend to him. She ached to help him, get him to safety. But the best thing she could do right now was try to keep him safe the only way she knew how. By leading the danger away from him. "Which way?"

The masked man pointed, motioning with the gun. "Go in front of me. Don't forget, I'll be right behind you. Try to pull anything and you're a dead woman."

Nina had a horrible hunch he planned to shoot her whether she cooperated or not. Yet she couldn't argue with him. Not when Mateo was only feet away, utterly out cold and unable to fend for himself at the moment.

Coco whined miserably but Nina didn't dare look back. She took one step then another. Her battered body seemed to gain strength as she moved.

They trudged through the woods. Nina was only vaguely familiar with this area. The hunting cabin was miles away, but the area was still very rural. If she wasn't mistaken, Mulberry Creek—which was more of a river, really—ran nearby. They had passed over it quite a ways back where it rushed under the road.

Every now and again, she felt something jab her back.

She knew it was the tip of the handgun and that he was taunting her with it. She kept walking, her heart pounding, her mind reeling. Was Mateo okay? Would this man stop at the vehicle on his way back? Was Mateo still in danger?

Probably. The realization terrified her.

"Are the items in the box really worth killing for?" Nina asked.

"You're not allowed to ask questions."

"Really?" Nina hated how her voice trembled. She did not want to give this man the satisfaction. "I assume you're going to kill me. What would it hurt if you answer me first?"

They came to a ridge. Nina could see the water flowing below. She knew then what he planned to do. He would shoot her, allowing her to tumble over. Her body would be carried away by the water. Would anyone ever find her? It was possible that they wouldn't.

Stop, she told herself. *You're not dead yet. You have a brain. Use it.*

Keeping herself as far from the edge as she could, she gave him an imploring look.

"Why are you stealing from the elderly? Why are you burying their treasures? Are you hoarding them for later? Or is it all for the thrill?" She was not going to admit she suspected he'd killed at least two people.

"The thrill?"

His voice had an edge and she knew she'd offended him. He gripped the gun but his hand had fallen to his side.

Keep him talking. Find a way out of this.

"That's how it looks to me. Like you're just in this for the thrill of it."

"You know nothing, you nosy woman. Why couldn't you just leave well enough alone? You stole from me!"

Stole from *him*? What about the people whose lives he'd infiltrated? He'd taken their precious items. He'd possibly done worse.

"You're the one that stole." She tried to keep the quiver from her voice. She did not want him to know how afraid she was. "All of the items in that box belonged to other people. You had no right to them."

"Because of you—" he waved his gun her way "—everything, *years* of planning, has been ruined. I think you need to pay for that."

Was there anything she could say to calm this angry killer?

Mateo came to with a jolt. His awareness that something was terribly, horrifically, wrong had snapped him back to reality. He stuffed down a groan as pain ricocheted through his head. He blinked hard, trying to clear his hazy, blurry vision. Nausea swelled up but he chose to ignore it.

"Nina?" His voice was hoarse, muted. When she didn't answer, he twisted his head away from the tree he'd found himself looking at through the spiderweb cracks of his window. Now he faced her empty seat. Horror filled him when he realized her door was open and he couldn't see her anywhere.

Coco whimpered and the sound terrified him because he knew Nina would not take off and leave her dog behind. Granted, she wouldn't leave him behind, either, but that thought took a few more seconds to surface.

Or would she?

Had she gone for help?

No.

In that instant, Mateo remembered they had been followed. Shot at. Someone had been after them. He had to assume that *someone* had taken Nina while he'd been unconscious. He wanted to yell in frustration, but that wouldn't help anyone. He reached for his sidearm.

Gone.

Of course it was. He hoped Nina had it with her for protection, but he doubted that.

The only way to help her was to get moving. It took him too long to get out of the vehicle, past the floppy airbags, and out Nina's door since his was jammed against the oak. He caught sight of his face in the side mirror. The amount of blood made him do a double-take. He quickly shrugged out of his jacket and swiped his face clean, then held it against the wound for a moment to see if it was still bleeding. It was a relief that it didn't seem to be.

Coco whimpered.

"Don't worry, little one." He reached for the back door and tugged it open. "I won't leave you behind." He released the dog from the safety straps that had undoubtedly kept her from harm. When he had her out of the vehicle, the spaniel wriggled in his arms. He placed her on the ground and watched as she trotted off toward the woods. She looked like a pup on a mission. No hesitation.

Coco was a therapy dog. She was *not* a tracker. Mateo knew that much. He also knew that she was a dog who loved her owner. When Coco took off for the brush, he followed, having no doubt that she was looking for her master. Realizing that, in his addled state, he'd forgotten her leash, he commanded her to heel.

The dog froze in place but gave him an imploring look, as if torn between wanting to be obedient and needing to race toward her beloved Nina. She didn't trot back to him but she did wait for him to catch up. Mateo realized Coco had stopped next to a shattered cell phone in a purple case.

It was Nina's, he knew. The phone looked broken beyond use; he grabbed it and stuffed it into his pocket anyway.

They got moving again and Coco obediently stayed close but was always a step or two ahead of him. He was okay with that. What he would not be okay with was letting her run off. If he lost Nina's cherished furry friend, she would be heartbroken.

If she's alive. He clenched his teeth and banished the thought from his brain. Nina was alive. She had to be.

Please, God.

As his head thudded in pain, and his vision remained blurred, it was the most articulate prayer he could scrounge up. The best plea he could muster in the moment. Yet he felt the weight of it, so heavy and intense it could have knocked him to his knees.

Maybe it should have.

Mateo suddenly felt the urge to drop to his knees and pray as he hadn't prayed in years. He couldn't do that, couldn't take the time. Nina needed him to find her. Needed him *now.* So he would pray as he ran—or more like stumbled through the woods.

He still felt lousy, weak, bleary-eyed. The throbbing in his head had not subsided, but he couldn't worry about any of that now. It occurred to him that he was blindly following a dog into the woods, deeper by the minute. What if she wasn't leading him to Nina? Was it possible she was just running?

When Coco stopped and sniffed the air then the ground and began to move again, he relaxed. They moved through the woods for what felt like forever, but he was aware it maybe only felt that way because he was in rough shape.

An angry voice reached Mateo's ears.

Then a softer, gentler voice. Nina.

Thank You, God. She's alive.

"Coco, come." His voice was low but firm.

The dog hesitated then reluctantly obeyed. Mateo scooped her up in his arms because it would do no good to have her race to her master's side.

He couldn't hear what Nina was saying, but it was undoubtedly her. He edged forward slowly, trying to be quiet. He felt awkward as an ox after the accident. And helpless. He had no weapon and held a squirming pooch in his arms. His coordination was questionable at the moment.

God, help us because I'm too much of a mess to help myself, let alone Nina.

He could see them now. A man dressed in black had his back to Mateo. Nina stood in front of him. The man waved his gun in the air.

"Stop talking!" he yelled, his anger reverberating through the woods. He raised his hand as if to pistol-whip Nina. "You nosy, meddling—"

Before Mateo could react, Coco leapt from his arms. She let out an angry bark at the stranger. The man whirled and the dog lunged at him, clasping the hand with the gun in her jaw. She held on tight, like the proverbial dog with a bone. Mateo was surprised she had that sort of feistiness in her, but he realized Coco was only protecting the person she loved.

Nina shrieked in surprise and ran to Mateo, calling for Coco to come.

Everything happened fast then. The man kicked at Coco but missed and she leapt away. The gun went flying when the dog released his hand. Mateo could see blood streaming from his fingers. The guy let out a feral-sounding scream as he clasped his injured hand with his good hand.

Nina broke through the tree line, Coco at her heels.

Mateo only briefly contemplated tackling the man, but he was not at full strength. Not even close after the rollover. Mateo couldn't see where the gun had landed. Was it at the man's feet, within easy reach? Best to go on the offensive.

"Run!"

Mateo let her lead the way, knowing neither one of them knew where they were or where they were going. They had one goal: to escape. He was determined to stay behind Nina, to put himself between her and a bullet should the man decide to shoot. He was about to tell her not to slow down because of him. Then he realized she'd been in the accident as well. That was probably why she wasn't moving as quickly as he knew she was capable of. He prayed they were moving fast enough.

He glanced down once and was satisfied that Coco was keeping stride with them. She had found Nina and was not going to let her out of her sight.

"We need to make a plan." Mateo, an avid runner, was embarrassed that his voice came out in a huff. His head was hurting fiercely and nausea swirled. He had a concussion, he was sure of it, though there was nothing he could do about it.

Nina glanced over her shoulder then slowed. Finally, they came to a standstill. He knew she sensed he needed a break. It was a blow to his ego, but he wasn't going to argue.

"I have a plan." She looked in the direction they'd been headed. "When he had me stand at the edge of the cliff, I noticed there's a footbridge up ahead. If we cross over, maybe we can lose him."

Coco whined.

They both glanced down. She was scratching manically at her neck and whimpering.

Nina frowned. "What's the matter, Coco?"

"She was doing that earlier."

Nina knelt and pulled her dog close. "Do you have a thorn? Did a sticker bush of some sort get you?"

He watched as she ran her finger around Coco's collar, looking for whatever was causing the dog discomfort.

"What is this?" Nina's brow creased as she popped off Coco's collar. "That's not a thorn."

Mateo knew instantly what he was looking at. A tiny black object affixed to the inside of the dog's collar. A small tuft of hair had come off when Nina removed the collar, having gotten stuck on the backside of the device. It had been tugging at Coco's skin, making her uncomfortable.

"That's a tracker." His gaze swiveled around the forest. Were they being stalked right now? Probably. "At Golden Acres, when she went missing—"

"That's how he followed us." Nina tore off the tracker, popped the collar back on the dog, and took off. "Come on!"

Mateo hurried after her, his adrenaline kicking in, helping him ignore the pain. When he spotted the footbridge ahead, he groaned. It was ancient.

They slowed.

"That doesn't look safe. I don't think we can cross."

She eyed him. "We can't. You must outweigh me by fifty pounds."

At least.

"But I can. And this—" she held up the tracking device "—has to. It's the only way to get him off our tail."

"I don't—"

He didn't have the chance to finish his protest. Nina hustled to the bridge. He understood her rush. Time could be running out. If this man was easily tracking them, he may only be a minute or two behind. Mateo assumed the guy had spent time looking for his gun or he'd be on their backs by now.

Or perhaps he was taking his time because he had a tracking device that would eventually lead the way.

A protest dangled on the tip of his tongue but he leaned down and grabbed Coco instead. Kneeling next to her, holding her collar, he began to pray as Nina crossed the wobbly bridge. It swayed under her weight. The weathered rope that held the planks in place looked frayed, worn. He could hear it creak. Groan. Moan in protest.

The water rushed below.

Please, God… The prayer, on a constant loop, filled his mind.

Mateo watched her cross, and his gaze drilled into her back as if he could hold her up by his sheer will.

She stopped halfway then whipped the tracking device across to the other side. It was so small, he didn't see where it landed, but he didn't need to know.

When Nina turned around, he realized how afraid she was. Her jaw was set. Her eyes were wide. She looked terrified yet determined. His admiration for her soared. Admiration and…yes, he could admit it to himself. It would be ridiculous to deny it.

He was falling for her.

He could hear the bridge complain continuously under her weight. *Please, God…*

She stopped when she reached the end and stepped onto solid ground. He rushed forward, ready to pull her along. But as she knelt, he realized she was taking something out of her fanny pack.

A small scissors.

"For gauze," she whispered. "Or a rickety old bridge." She opened it wide and began to saw away.

The urge to grab her and run hit Mateo hard, but he decided to give her just a moment.

Coco had stilled, her attention now on the woods.

Nina quickly moved to the other side of the rope bridge and did the same.

Coco growled.

Nina leapt to her feet. Her eyes large and questioning.

"I think he's coming." Mateo whispered the words as he scooped up Coco. Together they rushed into the thickest part of the foliage. They crouched down, making themselves as small as possible. Then they waited.

So much time passed that Mateo began to wonder if Coco had misled them. He placed the dog on the ground between them, where she sat obediently, as if she understood the gravity of the situation.

The brush to their left rustled.

Coco stiffened but remained silent as Nina held a gentle hand against her neck, holding her in place next to her body.

They watched as the attacker trudged out of the woods. He held the gun in a hand that was smeared with blood. In his other hand, he held a cell phone. He still wore his mask as he moved to a spot right in front of them. The man studied the phone screen then glanced up at the bridge. He hesitated only a moment before he made his way to the unsteady crossing.

Mateo realized the gunman probably assumed Mateo, who was roughly the same size, had crossed without incident.

The man took a step onto the bridge.

Nina reached out her free hand and latched onto Mateo's fingers, holding them tight. He squeezed back because it was the only support he could offer in that moment.

Their attacker took a step. Then another. Finally reached the middle of the bridge.

The bridge creaked.

Groaned.

Whined as if in misery.

Pop.

One side of the rope bridge gave way. The man let out a guttural yell and dropped to his knees. His phone and gun fell from his hands, flying into the water below. He gripped the wooden slats that made the walkway as—

Pop.

The other side of the bridge gave way and the whole thing swung toward the wall of the cliff on the far side.

He crashed into it but held on.

Nina let out a whimper.

The man was no threat to them, though he was climbing the slats of wood now that the bridge had turned into a makeshift ladder.

"Should we do something?" Nina whispered.

"It looks like he's going to climb to safety. The best thing we can do is get out of here before he sees us. Hopefully, he'll assume we've crossed to that side and look for us there."

They stayed hidden as they watched through the branches.

In a matter of minutes, the man had managed to scramble to the top. Once he reached solid ground, he bent over, hands on knees, his chest heaving as if he needed a moment to catch his breath.

"I think he had the scare of his life." Nina didn't sound sorry about that.

Mateo rose, pulling Nina with him. She was only an arm's length away. And then she was closer, in his arms, pressed against his chest. He held her tight as she trembled, and he wished he could wash all her fears away. Despite the wrongness of the situation, it felt right to have her in his embrace. As if she belonged there.

"I didn't want to kill him," she murmured, "so I'm glad he made it to the other side, but I don't know what it's going to take to get him to leave us alone."

Mateo knew that nothing short of death, or being caught, was going to get this man out of Nina's life.

TEN

Nina slipped from Mateo's arms as they watched from their hidden vantage point. The man looked right and then left, as if trying to decide which way to go. Without his phone as his guide, he seemed a bit lost. He had no way of knowing the now-useless tracking device was only feet away. He let out a howl of frustration and kicked at the ground hard enough to send dirt into the air.

Coco whimpered and huddled against Nina's leg. She bent and rubbed the dog's head in an effort to comfort her.

Take off your mask, you coward. The thought seemed to play on repeat in her mind. But her silent plea went unheard. How could they be so close to having answers, so close to catching this guy, yet so far away?

Now that he was safely on the other side of the river, they could easily take off back toward the road. Yet it seemed wise to let him believe they were on his side of the river as well. Let him go off on a wild-goose chase as he tried to track them down. She understood why they were staying put, staying out of sight, for now.

A moment later, still clearly furious, he stomped off and disappeared into the woods.

Mateo swayed. Nina reached out a hand to steady him.

"You hit your head. There was blood on the window. I

was so scared—" Her voice cracked as tears burned. His face was still a bit of a mess, though he'd clearly made an effort to clean himself up.

He slid a finger under her chin and looked into her eyes. "Hey, I'm okay."

She nodded. "You have no idea what a relief it was to see you come through those woods. He thought you were dead, you know. That's the only reason he left you behind. You looked like you were in pretty rough shape. He didn't question it."

"I hate that I wasn't there to protect you." His hand fell to his side.

"You did protect me. You came after me." She studied his face. "How are you feeling?"

"I'm fine."

"Now isn't the time for sugarcoating, Mateo. I'm a nurse, remember?"

He nodded.

She reached over and felt the lump on the side of his head. Her fingers came away with crusted blood. She opened up her fanny pack and took out an alcohol wipe to scrub them off. It was time to put away her emotions and act like the professional she was. "You need to see a doctor. Are you dizzy?"

He pursed his lips and didn't answer.

"Considering how you swayed, I'm going to take that as a yes. Nausea?"

Again, he hesitated, but after she shot him a disapproving look, he nodded.

"Any vomiting?"

"No."

"Blurry vision?"

He glanced away and she took that as another affirmative. "How bad?"

"It's getting better. It was pretty bad when I first came to."

She blew out a breath. He'd been knocked unconscious, had a lump on his head, and was suffering from nausea and double vision.

"You have a concussion."

"I know."

"You should rest, but that doesn't really seem to be an option right now." The sky was darkening and she was afraid another storm was moving in. They couldn't spend the night out here. She looked around, suddenly feeling disoriented. "We need to get back to civilization. Which way do we go?"

"Uh." Mateo looked baffled by the question. He eyed their surroundings. "I'm not sure."

"Your compass, Mateo." Her tone was gentle as she gave the reminder. Confusion was another sign of a concussion.

"Oh."

He lifted his wrist and stared at the watch, moving it close to his eyes then away again.

Nina bit her lip as she watched him squint, trying to make out which way the arrows pointed. She knew they had to head west to get to the road. It should be an easy hike as soon as they started moving. At least, it would've been easy under normal circumstance. She wasn't so sure now, with Mateo's vision blurred and his head concussed.

She gently reached out and clasped his wrist in her fingers. He gave her a startled look. The smile she gave him felt forced. Worry niggled at her, and she didn't want him to know. She didn't like the state he was in.

"Let me look." It took her only a moment to determine which direction they needed to head. She let go of his wrist but clasped his hand instead. He didn't argue and she was glad. She doubted he realized she was holding his hand so it would be easier for her to lead the way. It would do no good to have him stumble or stray.

It was slow going as they trudged out toward the road. Coco walked slowly behind them, as if she, too, sensed Mateo was struggling.

"I heard him yelling at you." Mateo's voice sounded strained and Nina assumed it was from pain. "Did he reveal anything?"

Disappointment zinged through her. "I tried to get him to talk. He didn't reveal anything. I couldn't even get him to admit to stealing the items."

"What *did* he say then?"

"He was furious that I stole from him and accused me of ruining everything."

"Right. It's a little bit harder to steal from the unsuspecting elderly once law enforcement is on to you," he mumbled. "I can't help but wonder how long this has been going on. The items that have been identified seem to have been stolen somewhat recently. But are there other boxes buried in the park? Or somewhere else?"

"I did ask why he buried the box in the park." She let out a little huff. "He told me it was none of my business."

"He's a real chatty fellow, I take it," Mateo said wryly. "I hope you didn't ask him about Gloria and Chester."

"No." Nina shook her head. "I didn't want to anger him. He was mad enough about the items in the box. I didn't dare ask him if he murdered someone."

Mateo stumbled over a branch and Nina's grip on his hand tightened. She needed to get him out of here. He needed rest, not to be making a strenuous trek through the woods when he couldn't even see clearly.

Coco whimpered.

"Do you need to take a break?" Nina asked.

"No." Mateo sounded annoyed that she'd asked. "I want to get out of these woods and get back to work."

Nina saw no point in telling him that was a bad idea. He wouldn't want to hear it, so she'd deal with that later.

"I need a break," Nina said.

Mateo gave her a skeptical look. She knew he was about to argue that they were not going to take a break on his account.

"I'm starving." Nina was telling the truth, not just using it as an excuse to stop. "I really wish we had some water."

"I could chug a gallon," Mateo admitted.

"I don't have water, but I do have a snack."

Mateo's stomach growled. "Guess I'm starving, too."

She unzipped her fanny pack and pulled out two peanut butter granola bars. She handed him one. "I wish I had more."

"Hey, this is better than what I have. Which is nothing." He tore open his wrapper.

Coco watched them with interest. Her nose twitched as she scented the treat in the air. Then she plopped her head down on her paws and looked forlorn.

Dog food was one thing Nina did not have with her.

She broke her granola bar in two, intending to share with Coco. Before she had a chance, Mateo had handed the dog *his* granola bar. The whole thing.

"Mateo!"

"What?" His eyes widened as he looked at Nina then back at the dog. "Oh, no. Was there something in there that she can't have? Something bad for her? I know a lot of human food is bad for dogs. I should have asked." He looked like he wanted to take the treat back, but Coco had gobbled it up already.

"No, it's fine. It's just that you said you were starving."

"I am. But so is she and she doesn't understand what's going on. I couldn't have her thinking we were being neglectful. You said that she came from a neglectful hoarding situation. I guess I thought maybe that meant she hadn't been properly fed. I didn't want her to worry."

Nina was sure she could literally feel her heart swell in her chest. "That is the sweetest thing anyone has ever done for me. Even if it was actually done for my dog." She handed him half of the granola bar she held, instantly noticing that he didn't lift his hand to take it. "Please. I'll stress if you don't eat something."

"Okay." He took the proffered snack.

It only took them moments to finish.

Thunder rumbled overhead.

Mateo glanced skyward. "Sounds like we're in for another storm. Hopefully, we can get back to the SUV and take shelter. It's not ideal, but I think it'll take our attacker a while to get back across the river if he even tries. At least now he's without a weapon." He squinted at Nina. "Speaking of which, what happened to mine?"

"He made me toss it along with your phone."

"I figured as much. That reminds me, I have your phone." He pulled it out and toyed with it a minute. As Nina suspected, her cell was hopelessly beyond use.

"We should keep walking." Nina would like nothing more than to allow Mateo to rest a bit longer but now, with another storm coming, it was more important than ever to find shelter.

"Coco was really something special earlier. I didn't get a chance to tell you this, but the second I let her out of her safety seat, she was on your trail. You know, I read somewhere that dogs can smell their owners from several miles away. When she took off after you, I wasn't sure how far you'd gone. But she was determined to find you. It's obvious she adores you."

"The feeling is mutual." Nina felt a wave of gratitude. "I saved her life when I brought her home with me. Today she saved mine."

Thunder rumbled again. Louder this time. And with it, another sound that was entirely incongruous.

"Did you hear that?" Mateo asked.

"Yes." Nina stilled a moment, canting her head to the side, straining her ears. The wind had picked up, but she was sure she could hear sirens in the distance. "Is that what I think it is?"

"I hope that means help is on the way."

The very thought got them moving faster.

Hope swelled in Mateo's chest. The wailing of sirens grew louder, cresting over the echoes of the incoming storm. They followed the sound as Coco now trotted ahead of them. He hated that he was so unsteady on his feet. Hated the feeling of inadequacy because, try as he might, he still could not see clearly.

"How do you think they found us?" Nina asked.

"Not sure."

Flashing lights could be seen through the trees, letting them know they were close to the road. The vehicles kept going, first one then another. He and Nina were hustling along now. So close to reaching the help that they needed. They broke from the forest and spotted the two cruisers pulled over less than a mile down the road. The emergency vehicles were parked next to a tan car. Mateo was certain it was the vehicle their attacker had been driving.

A third cruiser approached and slowed as the driver

spotted them. The car came to a stop and Officer Lainie Hughes buzzed down her window.

Rain began to fall then. Big, pattering drops.

"Mateo!" Lainie cried. "What a relief. Get in."

He and Nina did not need to be told twice. He rounded the vehicle and nearly collapsed into the front seat. Nina and Coco slid into the back.

"The guy that ran us off the road is out there some-where," Mateo warned her. "But I don't think he's nearby." He gave her a quick rundown of what had transpired.

When he was finished, Lainie radioed the two officers parked right up the road to give them an update. Next, she called for backup so they could check the woods in the area the man had disappeared.

Mateo waited for her to finish.

"How did you find us?"

"We had a call about a rollover spotted in the woods." Lainie went on to describe how a teenager was on the way to town to meet up with friends. "Her family owns this land, their house is right around that curve. First, she spot-ted the abandoned car on the side of the road. She slowed to be sure no one was inside needing assistance. Then she noticed there was another vehicle, with extensive damage, smashed up against a tree down the incline. She got out to inspect and realized the car was empty but there was blood smeared across the window. She called 9-1-1 and gave the license plates number of both cars. We realized real quick that the Tahoe was yours. The other vehicle was stolen. No surprise there."

"Where is the girl now?" Nina asked, her voice full of concern.

"As soon as we realized one vehicle was Mateo's, and the other most likely belonged to the perp, we told her to head somewhere safe. We've already received confirmation that she's back home with her parents."

That was a relief.

"Would you mind pulling up ahead?" Mateo asked. "I should assist Officers Rollins and Baker."

"I'm sorry," Nina said, not sounding the least bit so, "but *no* you should not. That's a terrible idea. You have a concussion."

Lainie cut a narrowed-eyed gaze his way. "You could have mentioned that."

Nina continued. "You should be resting and, instead, you just hiked through the woods."

He was grateful that she didn't blurt out in front of Officer Hughes that he had blurry vision. And that he'd been stumbling around. As her superior officer, Mateo felt she didn't need to know that.

"Now what?" Nina asked. "Do we go back to the hunting cabin?"

Mateo shook his head and immediately regretted it when he was sure he felt his brain slam around from one side of his skull to the other. He hated to admit that Nina had a point. He'd probably be more of a hindrance than a help right now.

"I don't think going to the shack is a good idea. We know he used the tracker on Coco's collar to follow us. While he doesn't know exactly where we're headed, he may be able to figure it out as there's not a lot of residences out this way." He pinched the bridge of his nose, fighting against pain and nausea, and willed himself to think.

Where could they go on short notice?

Certainly not back to the ranch.

His house? No. By now the perp had probably figured out who he was. Especially since he'd clearly been at

Golden Acres earlier where Mateo had introduced himself and had been asking questions.

"My place has a great security system." Lainie gave a one-shoulder shrug. "If you don't have another safe house in mind, you're welcome to stay with me. I've been putting in extra hours, so I'm hardly there. We can run to the shack to grab your things."

It was a generous offer, considering the danger they were in. Mateo was tempted to turn it down, but they were running treacherously low on options.

"Thanks, Lainie. I think we'll take you up on that." He shifted in his seat and tried to gather his thoughts. "There are a few things I'd like to take care of first. For one, someone needs to track down Tucker Holden. Find out where he was this afternoon. Better yet, have someone take a good look at his right fingers. Coco got a hold of this guy's hand when she realized he was going to strike Nina. I'm not sure how much damage she did, but there was a lot of blood. There would definitely be evidence of a dog bite."

He gave her an update on what had transpired at the nursing home. The discussion with the ladies, then Coco disappearing and their later realization she'd been tagged with a tracking device.

"That means our guy was at Golden Acres this afternoon." Lainie's voice rose in excitement. "Are there security cameras?"

Mateo was wondering the same thing and it would've been his next question for Nina, if Lainie hadn't asked it first. He glanced over his shoulder and shot Nina a questioning look.

"Yes, there are some. I'm not sure there's one in the area where we found Coco."

This guy was likely familiar with the nursing home, so

Mateo had to guess he'd chosen a spot where he wouldn't be caught on camera messing with the dog. However, that didn't mean a camera hadn't caught him somewhere.

"We'll need a warrant, but it's imperative we get that security footage. We also need to look into every male that was working this afternoon."

"That could be a lot of men," Nina said. "It's a large facility. There's medical staff, cooks, cleaning staff. It's a weekday, so there were probably supply deliveries as well."

He frowned. "We'll also need to look at the sign-in book in case this guy was just a visitor."

He didn't have high hopes that the book would be of any help. No one monitored the sign-in. It was just as easy to jot down a fake name as it was to bypass the registry and not sign it at all. Still, he didn't want to overlook any detail that may help.

"I'll let Chief Barsness know we need a warrant," Lainie offered.

He was about to protest when he felt Nina's hand land on his shoulder. She gave it a tight squeeze. "That would be very helpful, Officer Hughes. If I had my way, Mateo would be headed to the ER right now to be looked over."

He shot a scowl at her over his shoulder. He was not going to the ER. There was too much work to be done. They were getting close now, he could feel it. "I've been looked over. You said I have a concussion. I've had one before and, if I recall, there wasn't anything a doctor could do about it anyway. You already diagnosed me and I trust you."

"I'm glad." Nina flashed him a sweetly smug smile. "Then you'll trust me when I tell you that you need stitches. That gash is too much for a butterfly bandage. Whether you like it or not, you need a trip to the ER. The nurse says so."

Well, he'd walked right into that.

ELEVEN

Lainie pulled her vehicle directly into the garage and immediately lowered the door. The less her neighbors saw, the better. Mateo didn't want small-town gossip spreading that Lainie had company. It might be too easy to figure out just who her guests were.

Though law enforcement was scouring the woods for the attacker, the guy had had a head start. If he followed the river, he would be out of the woods by now. The main road was less than a mile from where the footbridge had been. Officer Rollins had met the Dawsons, whose daughter had found the vehicles. He had discovered they had built the footbridge years ago, when their kids were small, to get from their home to their favorite picnic area on the other side of the river. They were warned to be on the lookout for the gunman.

Officer Baker had retrieved Mateo's weapon and phone.

Mateo itched to be in on the investigation but Nina wouldn't allow it. They had made a quick stop at the hunting cabin to gather their things, including one last casserole from Julia and Coco's dog food.

Then they spent what felt like forever in the ER. But Mateo knew that the doctor had given him priority and stitched him up expediently.

While Nina had waited in the ER with him, Lainie had run into a store to purchase two disposable phones, one for each of them. It was the best she could do under the rushed circumstances. They had already set them up on the drive to the house. While the cheap phones were not ideal, it sure beat being without communication.

Lainie had been in touch with Officer Baker so they could stay apprised of the situation. As soon as she had Mateo and Nina settled, she was going back out to assist with the search. He hated being left behind but knew he had no choice.

Lainie led them into her house. It was cozy, with ordered piles of clutter scattered throughout. Mateo could relate. Working odd shifts, being called in for overtime, and being wiped out physically and mentally when you were home wasn't always conducive to the best housekeeping. Not that her house was messy. It looked more like organized chaos.

"Sorry, I only have one guest room," she said. "You'll find it at the end of the hallway."

"Not a problem," Mateo assured her. "As long as you have a couch, I'm good."

She checked her watch. "I still have several hours left of my shift. I apologize, the fridge is pretty empty. It's been a hectic week." She winced. "Not that I have to tell you that."

Nina lifted her mother's chicken and dumpling casserole. "Not a problem. We'll save you some."

Lainie smiled. "Thanks. I'll grab groceries at some point. Mateo, there's a linen closet at the end of the hall. You'll find bedding there. I'll set the alarm before I go and you can expect me back shortly after midnight, unless something comes up."

"Thank you, Lainie." Nina gave her a grateful smile. "It's gracious of you to offer us a place to stay."

"Don't think anything of it." Lainie motioned toward Mateo. "The detective here would do anything for any one of us. The police force is like one big family." She strode to the door. "Stay safe, you two. I'm guessing our perp has his hands full right now, but if something comes up, the department is just a shout-out away." She stopped in her tracks and whirled around wearing a guilty expression, as if something had just occurred to her. "Before I go, there's something I should probably show you. Follow me."

Nina placed the casserole on the counter as she and Mateo both lugged their bags along with them. Coco's nails clicked across the kitchen's tiled floor.

Lainie stopped in the middle of her living room. It took Mateo a moment to figure out what he was looking at. He blamed his rattled brain for the delayed reaction. "An evidence board."

Blocking most of the big-screen TV was a large chalkboard, held in a wooden frame, on wheels. It had been ages since he'd seen a chalkboard. This one was clearly covered with details of Nina's case.

Lainie winced, as if embarrassed. "Sorry. I know we have something similar back at the station, but this case has been weighing on me. It helps to clear my head when I can just get everything out." She motioned at the board. "Gran was a schoolteacher and got to keep it when she retired because they'd switched to whiteboards. Gramps saved this for me because I had so much fun with it when I was little."

Mateo chuckled. "What would he think if he knew you were tracking a murder suspect with it?"

She grinned at him. "He'd be proud, for sure. Gramps was a detective for the Seattle PD for two decades. He's the reason I went into law enforcement. Anyhow, this is what we know so far." She turned her attention to Mateo. "Have I missed anything?"

Mateo and Nina shared a look.

"The only thing missing is the new information from this afternoon." Mateo eyed a piece of chalk, his fingers itching to get everything updated.

"Feel free to add anything you feel is relevant." Lainie winced. "Or if you think this is stupid, feel free to ignore it altogether."

"It's not stupid. It's brilliant." Mateo was impressed with the information she'd included. She had a great attention to detail. "We'll update it and maybe later we can all go over everything together."

Lainie's eyes glittered with excitement. "Perfect. Now, I better get going." She took off toward the door again.

"Keep me updated," Mateo called after her.

"Sure thing," she replied over her shoulder. Then the door that led from the kitchen into the garage banged shut, announcing her departure.

Nina let the large backpack drop from her shoulder. She moved closer to the board. "That lady has been busy."

He nodded. "I'm impressed. I have a whiteboard similar to this in my office. It helps to see everything laid out like this. While we were at the shack, I kept details in my notebook, but it's just not the same."

Nina's stomach growled. "I'm still famished. The casserole from Mom won't take long to reheat. I'm going to pop it in the oven, get Coco settled. Then get myself settled. You should relax a bit. After we eat, we can go over everything again."

Mateo's new phone rang. He hadn't adjusted the volume and cringed at the blaring sound.

"It's Lainie." He had figured so before glancing at the

screen as he hadn't had a chance to give his number to anyone else yet. "Hey, there. Do you have news already?"

Nina's eyebrow quirked and she took a step closer.

"I just got word that Tucker Holden is missing."

"Tucker's missing? I'm putting you on speakerphone for Nina's benefit." He looked at the phone but it blurred. Nina reached over and pressed a button so he could continue the conversation. "Define missing."

"Chief Barsness went to his parents' house himself. He's not taking too kindly to the fact that this man has tried to kill you more than once. First with the explosion, then the rollover. When he arrived, Tucker's mom claimed he was in his room. However, when she went to fetch him, he was gone. Chief believes she didn't know he'd left. The problem is she couldn't recall exactly when she'd seen him last. Apparently, he's been spending a lot of time in his room since his visit to the station."

"This guy keeps looking guiltier and guiltier," Mateo said.

"His mom is sure he took off because he's scared."

Mateo fought down a groan. "That seems to be his excuse for everything."

"Could be true," Lainie said, "but I agree. He keeps making some very bad choices. I've got to go, but I'll let you know if I find out anything else."

They disconnected and Mateo placed the phone on the coffee table. He wanted to turn the ringer down, but didn't want to prove to Nina yet again that he was still having some trouble with his vision. He'd let it go for now.

"Mateo, I can't believe it's him." Nina ran a hand through her hair. "All we know for sure is that he put a note on your vehicle."

"Are you willing to stake your life on that?"

Nina bit her lip. Then shook her head. "No. I suppose not."

"I know you think I'm jaded, and maybe I am, but there's a reason for that." Mateo's tone had gentled. "I've learned the hard way you can't let your guard down. You can't let your heart rule a situation. Just because you want him to be innocent, doesn't mean he is."

Nina sighed out a breath. "You're right."

Coco made a whining sound deep in her throat that grabbed Nina's attention.

"You're hungry, aren't you? And I'm sure you need to take care of business. Let's go, girl." She pointed a finger at Mateo. "I know you won't rest. But at least try to relax."

"Sure." He wanted to agree but his mind was spinning. He really needed to eat. Then update the evidence board. After that, maybe he could follow the nurse's orders and relax.

Maybe.

"Mateo, you told me you would relax," Nina gently chided. She eyed him as he intently studied the chalkboard.

"I am relaxing." Mateo motioned to himself. "I'm sitting in a cushy recliner instead of scouring the woods for the attacker. I got cleaned up. I've been fed. We've updated this board with everything we know. We've tossed around ideas. I'm actually feeling pretty good."

She bowed a brow at him.

"I'm not lying."

She laughed lightly. "I didn't say that you were."

"I'm not exaggerating, either."

He winked and his teasing caused her heart to flutter.

"You do certainly seem to be on the mend."

"It was your mother's dumplings and your nursing skills. Thank you for finding me some ibuprofen and getting me hydrated. It's made a world of difference. If you're implying I should take a nap, that's not going to happen. I've never been a napper and that's not going to start today."

"I didn't say you had to nap. You need to stop straining your brain. What I really want," Nina said, "is for you to stop staring at the board as if your life depends on it."

He turned somber and she realized she'd said the wrong thing.

"*Your* life might depend on it."

Nina shifted on the couch, jostling Coco a bit. She hoped Lainie didn't mind Coco being on the furniture, but she really needed the connection right now.

"You know what? I know it's important, but I'm really tired of talking about this case. We aren't going to figure out anything more tonight," she said.

"You're probably right." He shifted in his seat and Nina noticed he no longer winced when he moved. "What do you want to do? See if we can find a movie?"

"I don't think I could concentrate on a movie."

"Same."

"Maybe we could talk about something other than this case," Nina suggested.

"Such as…?"

"Mateo, when this is over, would you consider going out to dinner with me? Or a movie? Maybe both?" Her words surprised her. She had been thinking about this though hadn't exactly intended to ask him. Not yet. But, really, now seemed to be as good a time as any.

He stared at her a moment, silent, and she wondered if his concussion was messing with his comprehension. Then again, they'd been having a perfectly logical conversation only moments ago. Yet he seemed confused.

She felt the need to clarify. "Like, on a date. Not tomorrow or anything. But when this case is solved. I'm guessing it would be a conflict of interest to start something now."

"Oh." He cleared his throat and frowned.

She did not take that as a good sign.

"I was wondering if that's what you meant."

Not knowing what to say, she just looked at him expectantly.

"Look, Nina, I'm flattered."

Her heart sank. "But…?"

"But…it's not a good idea."

She mentally tossed his answer around for a moment, trying to make sense of it.

"Not a good idea because I'm not your type?" Nina studied him quizzically. She had thought she'd felt a connection between them. She supposed it could have been one-sided, but she had been sure she'd sensed interest from him.

"You don't seem like the sort of person who is into casual relationships," Mateo stated. "Neither am I. But the crux of the problem is, I'm not husband material. In fact, I'd make a terrible husband."

"Says who?" Nina demanded.

"My wife."

Nina's stomach jolted. Suddenly, her feelings toward Mateo felt all kinds of wrong. "Your wife?"

She rewound her memory. Hadn't he said he wasn't married? Had she misunderstood?

He winced, though she didn't think it was from pain. At least, not physical pain. "Late wife." He paused, as if debating what to share. "I made a terrible husband. She told me so. I made a lousy husband for her and, since my lifestyle hasn't changed much—I'm still a detective, I still work awful hours, my head still gets tangled up in my job—I'm pretty sure I'd be a terrible husband still."

Nina was at a loss for words. He was widowed? His wife—deceased wife—had told him he was a terrible husband?

"That seems like a very cruel thing to say."

He shrugged but his tone turned wistful. "The thing is, she was probably right. It's the last thing she ever said to me. Right before she dragged our six-year-old twins out to the car."

Nina's stomach twisted. Mateo had children? Twin sons? Had his wife taken them away from him? He didn't seem the sort of man who would allow that.

"You have sons?" she pressed.

He was silent for a long time; his gaze seeming lost and far away. Her heart dipped because she sensed where this story was going. Coco whimpered, crawled off Nina's lap and trotted over to Mateo. She placed a paw on his knee and stared up at him woefully. After a moment, he patted his lap, a clear invitation, and the dog accepted.

A sound escaped his throat, somewhere between a sigh and a groan of misery. "This isn't something I talk about."

Nina wanted to tell him it was okay, he didn't need to talk about it now, but maybe he *did* need to talk about it.

"I'm a good listener, Mateo."

"I do feel like I owe you an explanation. Jolene and I had a fight that last night. It was one of many over the last years of our marriage. She said she was leaving me, for good. I'd just gotten home from work. Her car was packed with suitcases. She was furious I was late again, always tied up on a case. I thought she just needed time to cool off. I was exhausted, so I let her go." His voice trembled. "She pulled out in front of a semitruck just a few miles from our home."

Dread trickled down Nina's spine.

"The semi hit the driver's side. Nate was in the back

seat, directly behind Jolene. They were killed instantly. But Josh…" He pulled in a shuddering breath. "He made it through the wreck. He spent over a week in ICU. He didn't regain consciousness, but every day he held on, the doctors became more hopeful. *I* became more hopeful. I knew the road to recovery would be long. I prayed…oh, how I prayed…that he would come back to me."

"What happened?" Nina coaxed, her voice soft, comforting, full of compassion.

"A blood clot." Mateo cleared his throat. "A blood clot formed and broke loose. It stopped his heart. It happened so fast. I had gone down to the cafeteria for a sandwich. When I came back, he was gone. Just like that."

Nina's heart clenched. Tears welled behind her eyes and then a few trickled down. She wiped them away, not knowing what to say. Mateo's heart had to have been shattered. "I'm not going to ply you with platitudes. Just know, I am very, very sorry for your loss. I understand it had to be devastating."

"Devastating. Yes." He looked at her then. "I'm sorry if I led you on. Sorry if I made you think there could be anything between us. There can't be. I don't have it in me."

"You don't think you could love that way again?" she asked.

"I don't think I could survive *losing* that way again." He shook his head. "There's no way you can understand that and you're naïve if you think you can."

His words took her by surprise.

"Are you certain about that?" Her tone was calm but firm. "I assure you, I am well acquainted with the intricacies of life and death. I'm a hospice nurse, Mateo. I'm honored to have the job I have. I help people slip away from often-painful bodies into the glorious Kingdom of Heaven.

I do what I can to be sure their last days are filled with dignity and compassion. I lost my sister when I was fifteen. I was there, right by her side, when cancer stole her from us, sending her from this life to the next. I held her hand as she died."

Regret flitted across his features.

"I know. I'm sorry. That was insensitive of me to say. For the record, I don't think you're naïve. Far from it. I think you're vivacious and smart. Beautiful and determined. Young." He finally met her gaze. "I'm too old for you."

She hadn't expected that. "Really? How old are you?"

"I'm thirty-three."

She narrowed her eyes at him. "You're nine years older than me, Mateo. That hardly makes you ancient."

"Yeah? Well, some days I feel ancient."

"You've dealt with a lot."

"It's made me feel old and jaded."

"You can work at changing how you feel," Nina said softly.

"It's not that easy," he huffed.

"Few things worth fighting for are easy," Nina countered.

"I don't want to ruin you…the way I ruined my wife. When we met, she was lively and always looking to have fun. Because of me, she turned angry, bitter. She hated my job, hated when I was gone, hated that I had to take emergency calls. I can't blame her. Being married to a law enforcement officer is rough."

Nina leaned forward. "Were you an officer when you met?"

"I was."

"She knew what she was getting into."

"I think at first the uniform seemed glamorous to her.

Eventually, the novelty wore off. Reality set in, and it wasn't a reality that she appreciated. I knew how much she had come to despise my job. If I'd only quit one of the hundreds of times she'd asked me to."

Nina knew where he was going with this. "You can't live your life wondering what-if. Do you really think that would've made her happy?"

He shrugged. "I honestly don't know. I feel like she changed a lot over the years. I'm not sure anything I could've done would've made her happy."

"Then don't you dare blame yourself. Don't you dare feel like you weren't a good husband." Nina leveled her gaze on him. "Her unhappiness was not on you. We all need to be responsible for our own happiness."

He didn't say anything for a long while, simply sat there, stroking Coco.

Nina let him stew in his thoughts.

Finally, he looked up, appearing lost and forlorn. "I have a lot of baggage. Too much. Dating again has never even crossed my mind. I'm not good enough for you, Nina. I'd only weigh you down."

Nina stood and crossed the room to him. She pressed a kiss onto his forehead then scooped Coco off his lap.

"I don't believe that for one minute. You are a wonderful person, worthy of love. Sleep well. I'll see you in the morning."

With that, she turned and headed for the spare bedroom before Mateo saw the tears that were spilling from her eyes.

TWELVE

Nina sat forward on the edge of Lainie's plaid couch. Her elbows were propped on her knees and if she stared any harder at the chalkboard, she thought she might make it implode. All of Lainie's notes tied together so nicely.

Who was the attacker?

She wanted the answer to jump out at her.

Of course, it hadn't yet, and it wasn't likely to soon.

Though Lainie was supposed to have the day off, she had volunteered to do some investigating instead.

Earlier, she and another officer had delivered Nina's Trailblazer. Unbeknownst to her, Mateo had seen to it that the tires had been replaced. Now, with his SUV destroyed, Mateo had insisted on having it here in case of an emergency. It was tucked away in the garage, out of sight.

Now he was in the kitchen throwing together a peanut butter and jelly sandwich, one of the few things Lainie had ingredients for.

Oh, Mateo. Nina had been trying hard to concentrate on the clues in front of her but her mind continued to swirl back to Mateo and his story. While she had suspected he'd been through a lot, she certainly had not expected anything close to the story he'd told. He'd been married. He'd been a father. She had seen firsthand how horrific her sister's death had been for her parents. Mateo had lost two sons. They'd been so very young.

She could almost not fathom the depth of his pain. Nate and Josh. Her heart ached for Mateo.

The very idea that he wasn't good enough for her was ludicrous. But she'd awakened this morning with the realization that now was not the time or the place to discuss romantic involvement.

Solving this case had to be a top priority.

She heard Mateo's phone blaring from the kitchen. He really needed to turn that ringer down. He strode into the room holding his sandwich in one hand, his phone in the other. Coco trailed after him, licking her lips. She had a dab of peanut butter on her chin.

It was difficult to tell who Mateo was speaking with, so Nina sat patiently.

When he disconnected, he didn't keep her waiting.

"That was Lainie. She spoke with Al Crenshaw, the oldest son of Chester Crenshaw. The one you said made the accusations against his brother." Mateo waited for Nina to confirm with a nod then went on. "Your hunch was right. He stated he believes his brother stole the funds *and* the Rolex that's missing. He didn't want to turn his brother in, and he had no proof, so he let it go. Lainie showed him the watch we have on file and he was able to provide a receipt. Furthermore, she got footage from a neighbor's security camera. Someone is seen breaking into the house the night Chester supposedly tripped and fell."

"And Gloria?" Nina was curious about the other "accidental" death.

"Officer Hughes has been busy. She met with one of Gloria's three daughters. Not only was the pendant missing, a very expensive pendant valued at several thousand dollars, but also an extensive collection of sterling-silver cutlery."

Nina's brow furrowed. "Did they report that?"

"Gloria had been 'decluttering' her house—that was her daughter's word—for the past year or so. They thought perhaps Gloria had sold the cutlery and just hadn't mentioned it. However, she had three different sets and had promised one to each of her girls."

"Making it unlikely that she sold them."

"She touched base with Jimmy down at Junkin' Treasures. The sets never came through his store. He also reached out to some of the other pawnbrokers in the area and none of them were familiar with the sets, either. I can't imagine an eighty-two-year-old woman would travel more than a thirty-mile radius. That's what Jimmy's phone calls covered." He made his way to the chalkboard. After taking a bite of his sandwich, he started filling in the information they had just learned. "Jimmy did have an interesting thought. Real sterling silver, which this was, could be melted down. Just like he mentioned with the gold. It would sell for a good price. The amount Gloria had would have been far too much to fit into that box."

"You think this guy managed to have it melted and sold?"

Mateo shrugged. "I'm just saying it's a possibility. There are buyers out there interested in silver for the purpose of melting it down, so yeah, that would make it a bit harder to trace. We have no proof that's what happened. Not yet. It's just an interesting theory that Jimmy brought up. Furthermore, this daughter of Gloria's—she's the only one of the three that still lives in town—told Lainie that she's the one who found her mother. She said something odd struck her that day. When she arrived, the back door was ajar. According to her, her mother didn't use the back door. She didn't mention it, though, because she had no reason to think it was relevant. In the chaos of finding her mother's body after what she assumed was an accidental fall, she forgot about it."

"That's not proof someone else was in the house that night, but it does make it seem possible."

Mateo jotted a few more notes on the board. "I think the department now has reason to look into both deaths thoroughly."

"Has the department gotten the security footage from Golden Acres yet?"

"We should have it by the end of the day."

"You and Officer Hughes have been busy."

Mateo smirked. "If I didn't know better, I'd say she's after my job."

Nina's eyes widened. "Oh, no."

He chuckled. "She'd make a good detective."

"Does the department have room for another detective?"

"Not at the moment." He cleared his throat. "I've been thinking for a while that maybe it's time to make a career change."

She stared at him, speechless.

"It's just an idea I've been tossing around." He shrugged. "Back to the case."

They went over everything again.

While the Senior Center could be a possible connection, because of Gloria and Chester, the two also had a connection to Golden Acres. Gloria visited a good friend often, and Chester visited his brother almost daily.

This made the nursing home the one common factor with a connection to *all* of the items they'd found owners for so far.

"If Golden Acres is the place that connects everyone, does that mean Tucker is off the hook?" she asked.

Mateo finished the last bite of his sandwich and shook his head. "He's not off the hook until I see his right hand. Or better yet, until we have someone else in custody. Besides, he volunteers at the Senior Center. But we don't know for sure he doesn't have a connection to Golden Acres. I'm pretty frustrated with that kid for taking off."

Nina winced at his use of the word "kid" because Tucker was twenty-one. Only a few years younger than she was. Her heart dipped. Is that how Mateo thought of her, as a kid, too? Sure, she was only twenty-four. But didn't her life experiences count for anything?

Mateo was going a bit stir-crazy being inside Lainie's house all day. He was used to being out in the field, working a case. It was hard to do so from his colleague's living room where all he had was the chalkboard.

They were close to wrapping up this case. He was sure of it, could feel it in his bones. That's why not being actively involved at the moment was so hard to take. Mateo reminded himself that he was keeping Nina safe, which was more important than anything right now.

He couldn't leave her alone. While he could call another officer in for a protection detail, the thought didn't sit well with him, either. He needed to be with her to truly know that she was safe. Meanwhile he needed to trust his department was doing everything it could do to catch this perp.

Even worse, he felt awkward with Nina today. He was embarrassed that he'd shared his story with her. It was probably Coco's fault, the way she was all-comforting and whatnot. He shot an irritated glance at the dog, though he knew he really had no one but himself to blame. A part of him had wanted to share with Nina.

He hungered to have someone look at him the way Nina often did. Like she trusted him, admired him, maybe even adored him. That wouldn't do. And was exactly why he needed to put a stop to any misplaced feelings that may arise.

He had ruined his fun-loving wife.

He wouldn't risk turning Nina, sweet, joyful Nina, into a bitter woman.

Why had he shared all of that with her? Was he trying to scare her off? Maybe.

She was rattling around in the kitchen, doing the dishes or maybe trying to scrounge up something to make later for dinner.

Or maybe she was just avoiding him.

But no, that was not Nina's way. That was something Jolene would have done.

Don't you dare feel like you weren't a good husband. Nina's words from the night before whispered through his mind. *Her unhappiness was not on you. We all need to be responsible for our own happiness.*

Was that true? Would he ever be able to stop feeling like he hadn't tried hard enough? Like he hadn't been good enough?

With an effort, he pushed the thoughts away.

He was jotting a note down, the chalk screeching across the board in a way that reminded him of his grade-school days, when his phone rang. He'd finally turned the ringer down, so this time it didn't make him feel like jumping out of his skin.

Picking it up, he expected it to be someone from the station.

He didn't recognize the number.

"Detective Bianchi."

"Detective, my name is Hector Gomez. My wife, Maria, is a resident of Golden Acres."

Mateo's interest was instantly piqued. "How did you get this number?"

"I called the station. Someone there gave it to me," the man said gruffly. "Is that a problem?"

"No. It's not a problem at all. I was just curious." Mateo had asked them to give out his new number in just this sort of instance. "What can I help you with?"

"My wife, she was talking with her new friend, Mildred. Apparently, there was a discussion about a variety of stolen items. Would one of those items happen to be a collection of gold coins?"

Mateo's brow curved. "Why do you ask?"

Nina's gaze was on him; he could feel her curiosity like it was a physical thing. He didn't want to risk a break in the conversation by filling her in right now.

"I haven't told my dear wife that they've gone missing, but when she told me about this book of yours, I couldn't help but be hopeful. Would it be possible for me to see this book? I'd like to know if the Mulberry Creek Police Department is in possession of my collection."

"I think a viewing of the binder can be arranged."

"So you have them?" The relief in the man's tone was palpable. "You have the coins?"

"Can you tell me a bit more about them?"

"Gold coins." He paused. "In a black collector's book. Do you have them or not?"

One problem with having so many people view the photo binder was that Mateo wouldn't be surprised if someone came forward trying to claim an item that didn't belong to them. He inwardly grimaced, realizing he should give people the benefit of the doubt and not think the worst.

Nina was right. He was jaded.

The coins were not in a book. They were in a plastic zippered bag. But had they been in a collector's book when they'd gone missing? Could this man be the rightful owner?

"If the coins are mine, I'm sure I can prove it to your satisfaction," Hector continued. "I have receipts for some, but not all. I might be old, but my mind is still sharp. I was sure I hadn't misplaced the book. I didn't want to believe it had been stolen. Didn't want to believe he—"

The man cut himself off.

Mateo waited, his heartbeat kicking up a notch.

He heard a tapping sound come through the phone. Subtle, spaced out, but definitely a tapping noise.

"Are you still there, Hector? You said *he*?" Mateo prompted. Who was Hector referring to? "Do you know who the thief is?"

Hector let out a weary sigh. "I have my suspicions, but I don't want to say. Not just yet. On the off chance the collection in your possession isn't mine, I don't want to throw the young'un under the bus."

The young one? Could he be talking about Tucker, who was in his early twenties? To a man Hector's age, that would be plenty young.

"When can we meet?" Mateo asked.

"Other than visiting my wife, I don't have a whole lot going on these days. You tell me when works for you. Although, I'd appreciate it if you'd come to me. I have a bit of trouble getting around. I don't much like going to public places anymore. Not unless it's church or Golden Acres."

"What's your address?" Mateo asked.

The older man rattled it off. "Can you come now?"

"I can be there shortly."

"I'll be waiting."

The line disconnected.

"I sure do hope you have information," Mateo muttered.

"Who has information?" Nina gave him a hopeful look. "Do you have a lead?"

"Maybe." Mateo didn't want to be too confident. "Do you know Hector Gomez? His wife—"

"Maria. Yes, I know them. They're a lovely couple. Maria is a resident of Golden Acres. She has early stage dementia, and had gotten into the habit of wandering away from home. Hector has a bad leg, from a farming accident in his youth if I recall, and walks with a cane. He wasn't able to keep up with her, especially once she started slipping out of the house. He visits daily."

That was right. He had mentioned he had difficulty getting around.

Ah, Mateo thought, perhaps that's what the tapping sound had been. A cane hitting the ground in slow, measured footsteps. Yes, now that he thought about, he was sure that's what it had been.

"He heard about our visit and believes the coins belong to him. He asked if I'd come by."

"I'm going with you."

Mateo's lips quirked. "I didn't doubt it."

He hadn't planned on leaving her behind.

She shook her head. "I can't believe this person stole from Hector, too. He's the nicest man. Oh, what am I saying? They're all lovely people. We need to find out who has done this to them and put a stop to it." Her eyes widened. "Wait. You said something about him having information? What does he know?"

"I'm not sure. He wouldn't discuss anything over the

phone." Mateo didn't want to admit Hector had hinted at knowing who had stolen from him. He would wait until they had the facts.

Using his phone, he confirmed that Hector had given him the correct address. Next, he shot off a text to Lainie. He wasn't going to take any unnecessary risks and had promised his chief he'd let someone know their whereabouts at all times.

Nina decided to leave Coco behind. While usually well-behaved, she knew Hector wasn't steady on his feet. She did not want to risk Coco accidentally tripping him up.

After a short drive to the opposite end of town, they pulled up to a worn-down house that was surrounded by trees. The grass hadn't been mowed recently and Mateo thought maybe that was something he could take care of as soon as he had the chance. It had to be a difficult task for a man who relied on a cane.

"This is the place," Mateo said. "Looks like it could use a bit of TLC."

Nina gave him a warm smile. "When this case wraps, I'm game if you are."

"Absolutely."

They carefully made their way up the rickety steps. Mateo noticed a board was loose and knew that couldn't be safe for a gentleman who had difficulty walking. Yes, a fix-up day was in order.

When they reached the front door, it was open a crack.

"Mateo?" Nina whispered and pointed at the opening.

"Help me...please..." The words came from inside the house.

Mateo and Nina looked at each other in surprise.

"I've fallen," the wobbly voice said.

Nina lurched forward, shoving the door wide before he

could stop her. He lunged after her, spotting a frail-looking, gray-haired man on the floor. His back was to them and he was motionless.

Mateo always tried to be vigilant but some things were impossible to plan for. There was no way he could have guessed that a giant weighted net, a fishing net most likely, would be rigged to fall over the top of them the moment they shoved the door open and crossed the threshold. He tried to pull his weapon, but he felt instantly, hopelessly, tangled. The more they moved, the more entangled they became.

"Stop, be still," he ordered. "Only one of us should move at a time."

"Okay," Nina said, her voice breathlessly afraid yet trusting.

A man stepped from behind the door.

He didn't wear a mask. Did that mean he was confident that this time his prey would not get away?

The man was *not* Tucker Holden.

Nina gasped. "Conrad Greene."

"Oh, squirm and fight all you want." Conrad's voice was harsh and taunting. "It's not going to matter one bit."

"He's one of the cooks at Golden Acres," Nina blurted out. "Conrad, what did you do to Hector?"

Mateo lunged for the man and instantly felt the jab of a needle into his arm. Suddenly it seemed as if his veins were full of ice. He wasn't sure if it was the substance now flowing through him or if it was his fear coursing through his body.

"What have you done?" He ground out the words even as he tried to maneuver himself in front of Nina, to no avail. They were hopelessly tangled with every movement making their situation more dire. The syringe came toward her and Mateo growled in frustration.

"You ruined my fun, now I'm going to ruin yours. Permanently."

Nina let out a yelp when he injected her.

Hector Gomez, the real Hector, not the man who made the phone call, who was sprawled out on the floor, let out a miserable moan that Mateo barely registered as his mind became increasingly fuzzier. At least the man was alive.

"Please," Nina said. "You've stolen. But—"

Mateo didn't hear the rest of her sentence as he felt himself lose his fragile hold on consciousness. Tangled in the net, he toppled to the floor, only vaguely aware that he pulled Nina down with him.

The world went black and there was nothing he could do to fight it.

Then he blinked into bright sunshine what felt like an instant later. Only, it was clear time had passed. The rumble of tires on gravel filled his ears, and he realized he was in a moving vehicle. He blinked again, trying to gather his senses as the attack at Hector's house came crashing back through his mind.

Nina!

He twisted and saw her sleeping beside him.

No. Not sleeping. She'd been knocked out as well.

Though his mind was still hazy, reality seemed to settle in quickly. They were in the back of a small SUV. Was this Nina's vehicle? It had black leather seats, just like Nina's. Rock music flowed through the speakers.

It was easy to piece together what had happened. After the perp had knocked him and Nina out, he'd loaded them into her vehicle. Now they were headed…where? Perhaps the bigger question was what did the man have planned for them?

Absolutely nothing good. That was a certainty.

Whatever he had schemed, Mateo intended to foil it. He was awake and becoming more cognizant by the moment. Still, he didn't have a plan and he desperately needed one.

Please, God, help us out of this.

This time, the prayer didn't even surprise him.

Forgive me, Father, for distancing myself from You. I come to You humbly, in my time of desperate need. Not just for myself but for Nina. Please, help me to help her.

How? How could he possibly help Nina when his hands and feet were bound? He felt helpless but he refused to feel defeated.

He was a long way from defeated.

Nina moaned and her eyes fluttered open. She blinked then looked startled. Her eyes locked onto his and her face showed instant relief. He wished he could reach out to comfort her, hold her in his arms as he had the day at the river. That wasn't possible. Not yet anyway.

Shh. He whispered the word. It was to their advantage if Conrad thought they were still out cold.

She nodded in understanding, raised her hands to her face and scowled at the clothesline rope that bound her wrists. Anger flitted across her face.

He strained against his own bindings. Wrists and ankles, both trussed tight.

Nina's gaze cut away from her wrists and landed on a fleece blanket.

The back of the Trailblazer was small, leaving almost no room to maneuver, but Nina suddenly seemed to be on a mission. She squirmed closer to the blanket, reached out and tugged. It slid away, leaving an emergency tote uncovered.

What was this? Nina's vehicular version of her fanny pack?

Though her hands were bound, she was able to flip the

latch on the box. She tipped it over and supplies spilled out. Emergency food, a foldable shovel, tow strap, bungee cord, work gloves, flashlight.

Jackknife.

The contents had spilled with a clatter and Mateo cringed and held his breath. But the thumping beat of the music had drowned out the sound.

She gave him a triumphant look.

Gravel still crunched beneath the tires.

A new song spilled through the speakers. The man up front began to sing along, his voice frustratingly melodic.

How could he sing at a time like this?

Mateo decided to just be grateful for the extra noise.

He sent up a thank You to God, a constant loop of his sincerest gratitude. He also prayed that Hector Gomez was okay. The sight of the man lying on the floor kept circling through his mind. Had he been hurt? Or had he been drugged the way Nina and Mateo had? As soon as they got out of this predicament, Mateo would send help for the man.

It took some maneuvering, since his fingers were at an awkward angle, but he managed to open the blade of the knife Nina had rustled up. He glanced at her. Her eyes were huge, hopeful.

Once the knife was open, he realized, with his wrists bound, he couldn't twist the blade edge in the right direction, not while having a good enough grip to cut through the rope.

Nina nudged his foot with hers. When he glanced at her, she held out her wrists to him and lifted her eyebrows in question.

He nodded then reached awkwardly toward her.

The vehicle was bumping and jostling along now, apparently going down a rutted dirt road. He tried to hold the knife steady as he moved it toward Nina. With all the jostling, he was afraid of cutting her, but he had to assume their time was running out. He had no idea how long they'd been in the vehicle unconscious.

Together, they were able to position the blade so that it would have a clear cut against the rope. He gave a jerk with his hands and her rope fell free. She quickly untangled the dangling remnants from her wrists. Just as hastily, she cut him free. Their ankles came next.

It was an odd sensation, lying there. Free. But not free.

He quickly played his options through his mind. He could catapult himself over the seat, attack the guy. But what kind of road were they on? Lots of roads in this area were winding, edging along steep inclines. Or what if there was an oncoming vehicle and they swerved into the wrong lane?

He couldn't take the chance.

"Now what?" Nina's voice, almost inaudible, floated next to his ear, nearly drowned out by the music and Conrad's singing.

His voice was equally quiet. "Now we wait."

He flexed his hands to get the blood flowing.

Then he gripped the knife, hating the idea of using it, but grateful for the protection it would provide.

THIRTEEN

Nina fought down the terror that had enveloped her since the moment she'd opened her eyes. She concentrated on her breathing, calming her heart, and reminded herself she was not alone. Mateo was there.

And she knew God was watching over them.

There was no doubt in her mind that it was God who'd blinded the attacker's eye to the blanket and the gear in the back of the SUV. It was God who'd helped her and Mateo cut their bindings free.

He had brought them this far, she had to trust that He would bring them the rest of the way to safety.

It was difficult to wrap her mind around the fact that Conrad Greene wanted to kill them. She barely knew the man, had only seen him in passing at Golden Acres. He'd always had his head down, always seemed to fade into the background. She realized that would make it awfully easy for him to lurk and linger...and listen.

As much as she hated inaction, she understood why Mateo had said they needed to wait.

Ambushing the guy, though that was her first thought, could have disastrous consequences. What if he shot them the moment he realized they were awake? What if Mateo startled him and he swerved into oncoming traffic? Better to hold tight, knowing they had the element of surprise. They were awake. They were free.

Mateo was armed.

The vehicle began to slow…and Nina's heart began to race.

She felt Mateo stiffen beside her.

He took her hand in his, the grip firm and secure. Nina squeezed back, hoping he understood what his presence meant to her.

Too afraid to speak, she could only guess at what he planned to do. Because it's what she would do, had she been the one in possession of the knife. She'd wait until they parked, until their attacker opened the back end, and then she'd strike the unsuspecting criminal.

They slowed, then slowed some more. From this angle, all she could see was lovely clear blue sky and treetops.

They were somewhere secluded then, judging by the thickness of the foliage.

Not a surprise at all.

The unmistakable *click-click-click* of a blinker kicked in. Then they turned left.

What was Conrad's plan? Pull them from the SUV? Shoot them? Bury them in the middle of nowhere? If he killed them, would anyone ever find them? The thought of her parents going through the heartbreak of losing another child filled her with anger and sorrow.

Nina shuddered and blood seemed to pound through her veins, making every heartbeat echo in her ears. She didn't want to die. Not today. She had too much living to do.

She would tell Mateo that she loved him, whether he liked it or not. Because she did and she needed for him to know that.

The vehicle came to a halt.

She backed up against the side of the rear hold, trying to give Mateo room to maneuver as the driver's-side door creaked open. He scooted himself into place, ready to attack the instant the back of the SUV opened.

Any minute now.

Please, God...

She prepared herself for the moment they were faced with Conrad.

Only...

Suddenly the engine revved.

The vehicle leapt forward.

They were moving.

And then... Nina had the distinct feeling they were airborne.

She let out a shriek as she jerked upright in unison with Mateo.

What was happening? This was not right.

There was no one in the driver's seat and a wide blue expanse of water was racing their way.

"Hold on!" Mateo latched onto the seatback, and she did the same, though it did little to hold them in place. When the vehicle hit the water, the impact sent her flying upward. She smacked her head on the ceiling of the SUV. Blood filled her mouth as she realized she'd bitten her tongue.

That was the least of her concerns because it took only a moment to realize that water was seeping in. She glanced around, spotted Conrad on the embankment above as the SUV wobbled then began to fill faster. Conrad turned and walked away, likely satisfied his dastardly deed had had the desired effect.

He had sent them over an embankment, into a lake, thinking they were still tied up and unconscious in the back end. There was no way to open the hatch from the inside.

"We're going under," she moaned.

"Not if I can help it. Get up front." Mateo scrambled over the seat and Nina followed. "We're sinking, but not fast. The engine is still running though it won't be for long."

She heard the desperation in Mateo's tone and wasn't sure why the engine mattered at this point. It was then she noticed the board wedged against the gas pedal, but that's not what Mateo was after. He reached the driver's-side door and began buzzing the windows down.

The engine sputtered…died…and the windows stopped. Dead.

"We need to get out before water starts gushing in." He pointed at the passenger's-side window, down most of the way but not completely. As was the driver's side. "We need to do this carefully but quickly. It's important to balance our weight so we don't flip and roll."

Nina's heart hammered. Flipping and rolling while they were trapped inside with water gushing in would be deadly.

"How do we do this?"

She listened as Mateo shot out his plan rapid-fire. They each needed to slide through one of the open windows. He warned her that if water began gushing in, and the vehicle sank, they would be suctioned down with it.

Nina understood. The two of them moved as quickly as the unsteadily bobbing vehicle would allow until they were each perched in a window.

Mateo's worried gaze fastened on Nina's. "Can you swim?"

"Like a fish." Her wobbly voice betrayed her terror, despite her attempt at levity. The endless hours at the lake as a child, with her loving family, had turned her into a powerful swimmer. Still, she was terrified. Swimming was one thing. Escaping a sinking vehicle was quite another.

What if they went under?

Nina didn't even know where they were. From the little she had seen, she hadn't been able to make out their location. How would anyone ever find them? They would have no idea where to look. She and Mateo had been unconscious for how long? Several minutes? Several hours? She had no way of knowing. They could be half a state away from Mulberry Creek, so far from home that no one would ever know where to search. They may never be discovered in this watery grave.

Would anyone ever tie Conrad to their deaths? Would he get away with this?

That angered her almost more than anything.

All these thoughts flittered through her mind in a matter of seconds. Then the vehicle jolted. She hoped they weren't going to die, but if they did, she needed Mateo to know how she felt.

"Mateo, I—"

It jolted again. She gasped in horror.

"Go!" he shouted.

Nina shoved out of the vehicle, pushing up with her legs, catapulting herself through the window. In an instant, she was in the open water, swimming away from her Trailblazer. Away from Mateo. It took her only an instant to realize that he had not shoved free of the vehicle at the same time she had.

She stopped, treading water, desperately watching as the Trailblazer rolled then sank.

"Mateo?" His name passed her lips in a choked whisper. An urgent plea.

Please, God...where is he?

Mateo had waited a few moments too long before trying to shove himself from the vehicle. He had needed to know that Nina was free first before trying his own escape, because he was terrified that if he moved too soon, it would throw off the vehicle balance and drag her under.

Now, as he kicked desperately, he realized the opposite had happened. The SUV had gone off balance when Nina's weight no longer helped it to stay even. *His* side had dipped and water had gushed in the window, causing him to flip before he'd had a chance to flee.

He was dragged down, pulled into the murky depths of this unfamiliar lake.

The giant breath he'd taken seared against his lungs. The water felt tumultuous around him. His heart cried out for Nina. He didn't know if she was safe. He couldn't help her because he could barely help himself.

He felt topsy-turvy. His body heavy with his drenched clothes. He didn't know which way was up and panic began to set in.

No!

Please, God... Please help me...

The sense of peace that surrounded him in that moment was like being held by an old friend…or perhaps, more accurately, a loving Father.

He stilled himself, his lungs burning painfully now. Then he remembered something he'd been told at one of the many police force trainings he'd been to. Slowly, he blew out the breath that he'd sucked in before going under. He watched as the air bubbles seemed to float to his feet. He knew then that he'd gotten turned around. What he'd thought was up was down. With a few strokes, he managed to turn himself. He blew out the rest of his breath, fully orienting himself now. The bubbles floated upward and he began to stroke with every ounce of strength he had left.

His head broke the surface and he gasped for air.

He felt as if he weighed a million pounds with his wet clothes. Keeping his head above water was an effort. Yet he thrashed around, desperately looking for Nina.

"Mateo!"

He whirled in the water and spotted her some distance away.

Never could he remember such an intense feeling of relief.

He loved this woman. There was no denying it and he no longer wanted to try. He thought there was a good chance she loved him, too. He wanted more than anything to find out. And he would, as soon as they were free.

"Mateo," Nina said again as she glided toward him in the water. She wore a look of relief so pure, so intense, it made his heart ache.

"You scared me to death. I saw you go down and you took forever to come back up."

"I'm okay." He nodded at the land. "But we need to get out of the water." The heaviness of his clothes continued to weigh him down, and he knew Nina must have the same struggle, so they needed to get to safety while they still had the energy.

Silently, they moved toward the wood-covered shoreline. Not where the vehicle had gone over, because they would never make it up the embankment, but a bit to the north where the ground evened out. Every stroke was a struggle. Fortunately, they weren't very far from it. Relief filled him when his shoe hit the lake bottom. He found his footing quickly. He turned to Nina and held out a hand. She reached for him and he tugged her to him, her body easily gliding through the water.

"We made it." Her voice was weary. She found her footing. "Mateo?"

"Yes?" His heart hammered, partly from exertion, partly with relief.

She placed her hands on his cheeks and kissed him. Her movement was so quick, so unexpected, that he didn't even have time to respond before she stepped away.

"Let's get out of here," she said. "We don't know where Conrad is. He could be lurking."

"Right." He should've thought of that. And would've if her kiss hadn't chased every bit of common sense right out of his head. But he was thinking now, and she was right. "Let's move."

They trudged through the muck, through the weeds, and clambered onto the steep shoreline.

Mateo didn't want to say it, but he feared that Conrad was watching.

Stalking them.

He wouldn't have been surprised if bullets started flying.

None did.

He and Nina quickly moved into the thickest part of the trees before stopping to catch their breath. Trying to gather his bearings, Mateo studied their surroundings.

"This lake isn't familiar to me," he said.

"Where do you think Conrad went?" Nina's gaze scoured the forest. "I caught a glimpse of him walking away."

"I think he assumed he sent us to a watery grave and that he's in the clear." Mateo paused a beat. "Since we don't know that for a fact, I'm going to play it safe and presume the worst. We need to proceed as if he's lurking in these woods."

Nina nodded and, in silent agreement, they moved without saying another word. Cold, wet, and exhausted, they trudged through the woods, trying to step soundlessly despite their fatigue. They hadn't gone far before Mateo spotted a cabin through the trees.

He knew Nina caught sight of it at the same time because she stopped and gripped his arm, holding him in place. "Do you think they have a phone?"

"There's only one way to find out." They trudged forward until they hit the edge of the tree line. Mateo studied what he could see of the property. It was a small cabin, overlooking the lake. The lawn had been mowed, but not recently, making him wonder if it was a vacation property rather than a permanent residence. There wasn't a garage, only a small garden shed, and he didn't see a vehicle in the driveway. He turned to Nina. "Stay here. I'm going to get a better look."

Nina looked like she wanted to argue. Instead, she bit her lip and nodded.

Mateo crept onward quickly, feeling as though he was being watched, but wondering if it was just paranoia after all that had happened. He glanced over his shoulder, startled for a moment that he didn't see Nina, then caught a glimpse of her as she peered out from behind a large tree.

In seconds, he was trying the doorknob of the cabin. It was locked, which was not a surprise. He peered in through the window mounted in the top half of the front door. The door led into a small kitchen.

His heart leapt.

Hanging on the far wall was a phone. A landline, cord and all, was within his view.

"Don't move."

The words sent a sizzle of adrenaline down Mateo's spine, even before he felt the tip of a gun being pressed into his side.

"Conrad Greene," Mateo grated out.

"What is it going to take to get rid of you?" Conrad growled. "You should have died in the house explosion. You were supposed to be dead after the rollover. You should have drowned in the lake. Yet, here you are. Where's Nina?"

Mateo forced a tremble into his voice. "She went down with the vehicle. I tried to save her. I couldn't get her out."

"Put your hands up and turn around slowly," Conrad said. "I want to look into your eyes when you die."

Mateo turned, heart hammering, wondering how he was ever going to get out of this. His eyes widened and he had his answer. The moment he turned, he saw that Nina had sneaked up on them. She held a thick, stubby limb over her shoulder. Before Mateo could even process what was happening, she swung the limb at Conrad's head. The dog-bitten hand that held the gun flew up in the air. Mateo grabbed it and easily tugged the weapon from his injured fingers. Nina struck Conrad again, forcefully hitting him in the back.

He went down with a thud, hitting the ground hard.

"Stay where you are." Mateo's voice was cold. He leveled the gun at Conrad with one hand while managing to worm his way out of his belt with the other. He held it out to Nina. "Care to tie him up?"

"I'd be honored." She took the belt from Mateo and wrapped it around Conrad's wrists over and over, eventually tying the ends together, tugging hard to be sure there was no way for him to wiggle free.

Conrad squirmed into a sitting position and glared daggers at them. "What is it with you two? Why can't I get rid of you?"

"Why are you trying so hard to get rid of us?" Nina demanded. "We never did a thing to you!"

"You ruined everything." Hatred oozed from Conrad's

tone. "You should have just minded your own business. It never would've come to this if you would've just left me alone."

"You killed Gloria and Chester." Mateo tossed the accusation out there.

Conrad blinked at him in surprise, clearly caught off guard, just as Mateo had hoped. "The elderly have accidents all the time."

"You became adept at sneaking into houses of the elderly with ease." Mateo forced admiration into his tone.

Conrad smirked. "Mostly, they can't hear so well. They go to bed early. I've found they aren't usually handy with gadgets like door cams and security systems. I go in quick, get out quick."

"What happened with Gloria?" Nina asked. "Did you kill that dear woman?"

"I didn't really kill her." Conrad scowled at her. "She fell. I was sure no one was home. Turns out she was puttering around down in the cellar. She scared me as bad as I scared her." His tone implied he expected a modicum of sympathy for this. "When she saw me, she was on the top step. Guess I shocked the daylights out of her. She tumbled backward and that was that." He shrugged. "That old Mr. Crenshaw, he came out of nowhere, looking for a drink of water. Saw me going for his coffee can, the one I'd heard him tell his brother he stores his cash in. I knew he'd call the cops so—" he grimaced "—I guess we had a bit of a tussle. He hit his head. No one questioned when Gloria fell. I figured no one would question when old Crenshaw fell. I was right."

"Why bury the valuables?" Mateo asked.

Conrad scowled. "I don't appreciate how nosy you are. I'm not going to answer that."

"Golden Acres is the connection," Nina said. "You work in the kitchen. You don't really chat people up, but I'm sure it's easy enough to drift around the place, overhearing conversations." She didn't wait for a reply. "Gloria and Chester both visited the Senior Center, but that was a coincidence."

He shrugged. "It bought me some time when I heard cops were looking into someone else. That Senior Center volunteer."

"Tucker Holden," Nina supplied.

"All of your victims had ties to Golden Acres," Mateo said.

"No point in denying that." Conrad shrugged. "Chester came to visit his brother almost daily. They'd reminisce about the tough old days. Living through the Great Depression. Chester let it slip that he still didn't trust banks. I happened to be delivering a meal tray to his brother. He also had this Rolex that his highfalutin son gave him. Yammered about it all the time. I figured at his age, he didn't need it. The watch, or the cash. And his son sure didn't, so what difference did it make if I took it? Gloria yammered on and on to her friend about the collections she had. Rose Medallion china, Carnival glass, an antique doll collection, which I did not touch."

Apparently, he'd only stolen the sterling silver.

"And the others?" Nina demanded.

Conrad shrugged. "Yeah, so I took a few belongings. There was still plenty left for their families to fight over. But what about me? I got nothing. My whole life I've been cheated out of what I deserve, what should be mine. My parents have nothing and that's exactly what they've passed down to me. *Nothing*. Joined the army but didn't get the promotion I wanted. My superior officer said I had an attitude and didn't take direction well. Had a good job out in the oil fields but they let me go because some guys wouldn't stop picking fights with me. My wife took off with another guy. Nothing ever goes my way!" he growled. "I was just evening the playing field a bit."

He spoke with such audacity. As if the world owed him. As if these elderly people, who had likely worked hard their entire lives, owed *him*. Conrad's utter lack of remorse left Mateo feeling equal parts revulsion and anger.

"The people I took from were old. They had no use for those things. Or, at least, they wouldn't soon."

Mateo did not feel it was even worth mentioning the obvious, that Conrad had no right to the items. Most of these people had family who would inherit the keepsakes.

"How did we end up *here*?" Nina held her hands up, motioning to the cabin.

He sneered. "Those old people do like to talk. Heard Mildred saying that it was a shame her son didn't use the family cabin very often, but that he was too lazy to clear it out to sell it. It was just sitting empty. At first, I thought maybe I could use it as a hideout, if things got to squirrely back in Mulberry Creek. Came out here to see it for myself. That's when I noticed that it had a nice, clear overlook of the lake."

Mateo noticed now what he hadn't noticed before. Tire tracks through the tall grass. This is where he'd launched the Trailblazer from. From where they stood, they had a lovely view of the lake, but they were looking at it from a slight elevation.

"You were going to drown us in the lake, then what? Just live in the cabin overlooking our graves?" Nina demanded.

"Hardly." Conrad shot her a condescending look. "As soon as I scoped out this place and ironed out my plan, I stored a motorcycle in the shed. After I ditched your bodies, I was going to ride back to Mulberry Creek and no one would be the wiser. But when I was fidgeting around, trying to get it started, I spotted this guy through the window." He looked at them in disgust. "That tranquilizer was supposed to last longer than it did. But I ended up splitting it three ways. Hadn't planned on using it on Hector. Was just going to ensure he took a fall down his front steps, but decided that might be one fall too many. Instead, I was able to sneak up behind him. He never saw me coming. At his age, I figured he'd wake up groggy, confused, and none the wiser."

"You impersonated him." Mateo scrubbed a hand through his hair. He felt so gullible.

"Why, yes, yes I did." Conrad's voice mimicked an older man's. "You were so hungry for information it worked."

"Nina, I think it's time you made a phone call." Mateo stepped toward the door and, using the butt of Conrad's gun, he smashed a hole in the windowpane, knowing he would replace it later. From there, it was easy to reach inside and turn the lock. This was an emergency and he was sure Mildred would understand their need for a break-in.

"I'll gladly make that call," Nina said. "It's time we put this nightmare behind us."

FOURTEEN

Mateo gripped the steering wheel of the rental vehicle he was using until his insurance claim was settled and he could buy something new. The driveway leading into Big Sky Ranch was long and winding. For once, it was nice to be heading there with good news.

His body ached and he was tired. Deep, down-to-his-bones tired, but in a good way. This case was wrapping up. Nina's ordeal was over. She was safe. He was no longer tasked with protecting her. At least, not in a professional way.

A frisson of hope washed over him.

Could he have a future with Nina?

He knew he was getting ahead of himself, but the thought of spending the rest of his life with her filled him with joy. She was the brightest ray of sunshine, bursting through the dark, dreary abyss he had been so lost in.

She had made him feel things he hadn't felt in years. Hope. Joy. Love.

Most important of all, he felt his faith growing, stirring, strengthening by the day. She had lost a loved one and she had become strong and courageous, not in spite of it, but because of it.

Nina was young, yes, but he was embarrassed that he had called her naïve. If anyone was naïve, it was him. He'd been unreasonable in his way of thinking. Closed-minded. And she had opened up his mind to all that he'd been missing.

The depth of her faith had reawakened his own.

Thank You, Lord, for bringing us through this ordeal. Thank You for helping me to catch Nina's attacker. Most of all, thank You for loving me and guiding me even when I was too stubborn to admit I still needed You.

He did need God. He needed Nina, too. Finally, he was ready to admit it.

As he rounded the last bend in the gravel drive, he slowed. Nina had asked him to come for dinner. She had warned it would be a large family affair.

He parked near the barn, out of the way of the two children who were playing some type of game in the yard. Mateo glanced around at Nina's loud, boisterous family as he exited the vehicle and strode toward the main ranch house. It had been so long since he'd been at a gathering like this.

Nina's father, James, and Eric, her oldest brother, were on the deck, grilling burgers. Her mother, Julia, and sisters-in-law, Cassie and Holly, were placing tablecloths on picnic tables. Seth, Nina's other brother, was setting up a game of cornhole for Wyatt and Chloe.

It made him miss his family, his parents and sister Mara. He promised himself he'd visit them soon.

Maybe, if the future played out the way he prayed it would, he'd bring Nina along for the visit.

Nina came out of the front door carrying a pitcher of lemonade. Her face lit up brighter than sunshine after a storm. "Mateo!"

She hurried down the steps and placed the beverage on the table before rushing over to him. Clasping his hand in hers, she beamed at him. "I'm so glad you decided to join us. I wasn't sure if you would."

"I thought your family would like an update on Conrad." His gaze darted around. Her entire family seemed to have stopped what they were doing and were watching the two of them with curious smiles on their faces.

Nina arched a brow at him. "I hope that's not the only reason you stopped by."

It wasn't. He had missed her. In the last twenty-four hours, while he had wrapped up this case and she had gone back to her family, he'd realized he couldn't live without her. Absolutely did not want to even try.

With her loving family nosily looking on, he decided this was not the ideal time to pour out his heart to her. That could come later.

"Do you have an update on Hector?" Nina asked.

He wasn't surprised that she would want to know. After their rescue yesterday, emergency services had been dispatched to Hector Gomez's house and care had been rendered. "He spent the night in the hospital, but should be able to go home today. His son is coming to stay with him for a few days to be sure he's doing okay."

Nina's tension visibly eased at the news.

"Mateo, so nice to see you." Julia walked up to him and pulled him into a hug. "We're so happy you could make it."

"Thank you for inviting me."

Julia's eyes sparkled. "Of course. After all you've done for us, not just with Nina, but Eric and Seth as well, you're practically family."

The sentiment caused a lump to form in his throat. Family. He realized now how much he had longed for family. Not just his parents and sister, but a family to spend each day with, to call his own.

"Mom—" Nina placed a hand on her arm, a clear distraction technique "—is there anything else in the house you'd like me to get?"

Julia shook her head as Cassie and Holly approached. "Not yet, but I do believe that we would all like an update. Mateo, do you have any news for us?"

"I do."

Seth quickly got the kids settled in with their game, then the adults gathered on the deck where James could keep watch of the grill.

All eyes were on Mateo.

"We've done a little digging into Conrad Greene's past. Seems he has a problem with anger management. He's had a hard time keeping a job over the years. After interviewing him, he blames his troubles on just about everyone and everything other than himself." Mateo's eyes met Nina's. "It seems he felt he was entitled to the items he stole, high-value goods."

"That scoundrel." Julia scowled. "Stealing from the elderly."

"*Murdering* the elderly," Holly added.

Mateo held up his hand. "He claims he didn't kill Gloria. He's backtracking on admitting to shoving Chester, but we have surveillance video proving he was there that night. We'll be able to build a good case. We're getting more information by the day."

"That's why he went after Nina." Cassie eyed the baby monitor that rested on the deck railing. One of the twins whimpered then hushed again. "He knew she may be able to connect the items she found to the people they were stolen from. And from there, he was justifiably concerned the suspicious deaths would come to light."

"Did he tell you why he buried the box in the park of all places?" Nina asked.

"No, but I interviewed his sister and she gave me some valuable insight. The two aren't close, according to her, but she does try to stay in touch with him. She visited Conrad a few weeks ago and accidentally came across his stash of goods. When she questioned him on them, he claimed he'd purchased everything. Said he'd started visiting flea markets and pawn shops and was hoping to make a profit on the goods."

Mateo shook his head. "She didn't believe him, but had no way to prove it. Regardless, she believes he buried them in the park to keep them from her. Said he wouldn't have gotten a safe-deposit box because banks have security cameras. He rents a trailer house and doesn't have any property of his own. Her hunch is that he was going to continue acquiring the valuables for as long as he could. Probably until he lost his current job. Then he'd take off for somewhere far from here and cash everything in."

"Far away where no one would be looking for it," Cassie said.

"Conrad's been pretty tight-lipped, but I have to say her hunch sounds pretty solid to me." Mateo met Nina's gaze for a moment. "His sister said he has a habit of jumping from one job to another. Taking off long stretches of time in between. Months. One time, more than a year. He's worked in nursing homes on and off for a decade."

He saw Cassie's eyes widen and knew her private investigator brain had kicked in. "The elderly are easy targets, sadly. Do you think this is a pattern? Are you going to look into his past employers? See if there are any other suspicious deaths? Or signs of theft?"

"Yes to all of the above." Mateo nodded gravely. "We do

have reason to believe this is a pattern. The theft at least. Whether there are other suspicious deaths…well, we'll look into that, too."

"What happens now?" James asked.

"Now, at a minimum, he's being charged with theft and attempted murder." Mateo's voice hardened as he thought of how the man had almost killed Nina, and him, when he'd blown up her house. "Once the investigation into the other two deaths is wrapped up, we'll know if we can add two more charges."

Truth be told, he thought by the time this was over, the charges against Conrad Greene might be as long as the man's arm. They had obtained the surveillance video from Golden Acres. While the cameras hadn't picked up Conrad bribing Coco with food, they were able to verify that he'd been working there that day.

"Regardless," Holly said, "he'll be locked up. Hopefully, for a very long time."

"We all thank you," Eric said, "for a job well done. It couldn't have been easy watching out for this rug rat—" he reached over and ruffled Nina's hair "—but you did good."

She laughed and ducked out from under him, effectively lightening the mood after such a grim discussion.

A wail burst through the baby monitor.

Eric winced then spun, calling over his shoulder. "I better get her before she wakes her brother. I'll be right back." He disappeared into the house.

"The burgers will be done soon," Julia said. "Ladies, should we grab the food?"

The trio of women followed Julia into the house. A moment later, they traipsed out carrying bowls and platters to the side-by-side picnic tables.

Mateo found himself alone with Nina's father.

He pulled in a breath, stealing himself. He'd wanted this exact opportunity, a moment alone with James, but now that he had it, he was as nervous as a teenager.

"Mr. Montgomery?"

The man turned to him. "Something on your mind, Mateo?"

"Yes, sir."

James's brow arched. "Sir? I think we're on a first-name basis after all of this. Call me James."

Mateo nodded. "I will. I have a question for you."

Nina's father placed the metal spatula on the side of the grill and turned his attention to Mateo. "Ask away."

"I really admire your daughter. She's smart, funny, empathetic, and so full of enthusiasm for life."

James chuckled. "I think you nailed that description."

"I would like your permission to date her."

"I was hoping you were going to ask that." James grinned. "Considering how starry-eyed you make her, I wouldn't dare tell you no." His grin faded. "In all seriousness, I admire you, Mateo. You have a tough job and you do it well. You took good care of my girl. I've known you for over a year now. I think you're one of the most genuine, trustworthy men I know. I can't think of anyone I'd rather see my daughter with. It would be a blessing to see you two together. Hopefully, for the long haul."

James's words were so heartfelt, so firmly spoken, that Mateo felt the weight of them down to his marrow.

"Your blessing means a lot to me." He cleared his throat and forced a smile. "Hopefully, Nina shares your sentiment."

"Only one way to find out." James nodded toward the yard where Nina was chasing after Chloe and Wyatt. "Go talk to her. I think now's as good a time as any."

"I'll do that. Thank you, James."

"Pleasure's all mine."

Mateo descended the steps, his eyes on Nina as she caught Chloe, pulled the beanbag from her hand and began tickling her. Wyatt crashed into them and beanbags went flying as the trio laughed uproariously.

"Mateo, wait up!"

He pivoted as Cassie hustled to catch up to him. She wore a wry smile. "Have a minute?"

A quick glance at Nina confirmed she was still busy with her niece and nephew. It wouldn't hurt anything to wait a while longer before talking to her. "Sure. What's up? Have a case you want to consult on?"

It wasn't an unreasonable guess. He and Cassie had bounced ideas and information off each other in the past.

"Not exactly." Cassie's smile slipped and she was all business now. "You know, Detective, I heard a rumor that you might be in the market for a new job."

He narrowed his eyes at her. "Maybe. What of it?"

"I happen to have an offer for you." Cassie grew serious. "Ever since I helped Eric with the case involving Wyatt's mom, I've been getting more cases thrown my way than I can handle. I have emails coming in daily. You know my specialty is reuniting family members."

He nodded. He knew Cassie had become a private investigator after a long search had led to her birth mother. She had wanted to help others who were in similar situations reunite with long-lost relatives. She was very good at her job.

"Some of the other stuff—" she wrinkled her nose "—I'm not really interested in. I've had some inquiries about cold cases, tracking down swindling business partners, and there's always requests to catch cheating spouses. You get the idea."

"Right." He knew Cassie liked the feel-good cases. And she had every right to pick and choose the cases she was willing to dive into. "That heavier stuff is not really your thing."

"No." She looked at him hopefully. "But I'm thinking it might be yours. Now that we have the twins, I want to cut my workload down, but the requests are coming in faster than ever before. Have you thought of becoming a private investigator? You could choose the cases you're interested in, set your own hours. You can work as much or as little as you choose, but, trust me, I have plenty of potential clients that could keep us both busy."

Set his own hours? Choose how heavy his workload would be? Decide whose case he'd like to dive into?

He had become a detective because he'd felt it was his calling to help people. But after more than a decade in law enforcement, he was ready for something new. There were other ways to help people. Cassie was proof of that.

Mateo leaned toward her. "I'm interested. Tell me more."

Nina watched Mateo and Cassie from a distance. Curiosity nipped at her, but she wanted to respect their privacy. Maybe Cassie was asking Mateo for help on one of her cases. She knew they consulted with each other on occasion. She also knew Cassie had her hands full with work right now. Her sister-in-law had commented that the requests were piling up and she couldn't keep up with them all. While she was proud of Cassie for building such a successful business, Nina knew it stressed her out to not be able to help everyone.

She took the cover off the potato salad as her mother came out of the house with a platter of buns.

Her dad took that as his cue and started piling burgers onto plates.

Mateo and Cassie wrapped up their conversation when Eric came out of the house with Ethan in his arms. Matilda must still be sleeping, though Nina doubted the parents would get a reprieve for long.

She saw Mateo glance at the child in Eric's arms, his face lighting in a smile. Nina had wondered if it would be hard for him to be around the twins, but judging by the look on his face, the baby brought him joy.

Once he helped James carry the platters of burgers to the table, they all sat.

After James said grace, the table filled with lively conversation. Nina enjoyed watching Mateo interact with everyone she loved the most. Yet she was anxious to have him all too herself.

When the meal was over, everyone began to help with clearing the picnic tables.

Her mother pulled her aside. "You've had a tough week. Why don't you and Mateo take a walk?"

Nina was about to protest because it was the polite thing to do. Before she could, Julia gave her a wink and a nudge. "Go."

Nina didn't need to be told a third time. While her family moved around, she sidled up to Mateo as he was about to grab the empty burger platter. She reached for his hand, lacing her fingers with his.

He gave her a startled look.

"Let's go for a walk."

"The tables aren't cleared," he said. "Shouldn't we—"

"*Go*," Julia said as she walked past them.

"Don't want to argue with my momma, now, do you?" Nina grinned at him.

He grinned back and shook his head. "I sure don't."

She led him toward the trail in the woods. It seemed the obvious place to head because she didn't want to stand in the yard with her family gawking at them. As it was, Nina was sure she could feel their curious gazes burning into their backs. No way was she going to look over her shoulder to find out.

"I hope my big noisy family isn't too much for you."

He smiled and shook his head as they reached the path. "After the week we've had, I think your big noisy family is just what I need."

"Water balloon fight!" Wyatt yelled, his voice carrying through the trees.

Chloe let out a shriek of laughter then Seth yelled, "Run! Run as fast as you can!"

Mateo chuckled. "Sounds like we got out of there just in time." His expression turned wistful. "I miss that. Kids' laughter. There's just something so special about it."

"Yeah, there is." Nina gave his hand a squeeze. She hoped one day he would share stories of his boys with her, but thought maybe it was too soon for that. In time, though, she prayed she and Mateo would have the sort of relationship where they shared everything.

They walked in silence for a while. She stopped once they were halfway down the trail that led between her parents' home and Eric's. The thick foliage kept them from prying eyes. Right now, Nina wanted Mateo all to herself. It was time they had the talk she'd promised herself they would have if they survived.

God had given them another chance at life. Nina was going to embrace every single day.

Mateo chuckled as he glanced around. "I'm pretty sure this is the exact spot I caught up to you the night you crept out of the house. I still can't believe you were going to take off without telling me."

"Honestly, I'm so glad you caught me," Nina said. "The past week has been such a whirlwind. I'm so grateful I had you by my side. You protected me, took care of me, and trusted me to be a part of the investigation."

"I don't know that I could've stopped you."

She laughed at that. "True." Then she grew serious. "I was going to say something to you while the SUV was going under."

"I remember." He shot her a curious look but said nothing more.

"I love you." Her words were matter-of-fact. "There. I said it. You can't make me take it back."

He chuckled. "Do you really think I'd make you take it back?"

"I thought you might. Or I thought you would remind me again that we're too different. That you're told old. Maybe tell me one more time that you've become too jaded because of your job." She narrowed her eyes at him. "So, are you going to tell me any of those things?"

"Nope." His eyes sparkled and he flashed her a heart-stopping grin. "I've had a lot of time to think about how wrong I was."

Had he actually admitted he was wrong? Wrong about why they couldn't have a relationship? Her heart leapt with hope and her eyebrows shot up in surprise.

"You see, you've been good for me. You reminded me that I have a lot of life left. I don't need to be a grumpy workaholic. You've reawakened my faith, and I believe that God led you to me, maybe for that exact reason."

Nina felt tears prickle at the backs of her eyes. She blinked hard to hold them at bay.

"In such a short time, you've changed my life in the best way possible. You've made me want to be a better person. A happier person. For the first time in years, I want to open myself up to love again. Maybe," he spoke softly, "even have a family again someday."

"What exactly are you saying?" She wanted to be sure, completely positive, that they were on the same page.

"You need me to spell it out for you?"

She nodded. "Yes, I do."

"I love you, too, Nina."

"I was really hoping you would say that."

He cupped her face in his hands, looked into her eyes, her heart, her soul. With a seriousness that could leave no doubt, he made a promise. "I love you. Now. And forever."

He kissed her then. Not a searing kiss, but the sort of kiss that filled her heart to bursting. It shook her down to her soul, lifted her hopes and dreams to the heavens. She had never known a love so deep, so strong, so full of promise.

"You know what, Mateo?" Her voice was a breathy whisper, full of emotion, but sure. "You're going to marry me someday."

"You think so?" His tone held a gentle teasing.

"Maybe not anytime soon," she admitted.

He winked. "True. We have a lot of courting to do."

"Careful, you're sounding like an old man," she teased.

He looked serious. "Our age difference doesn't bother you?"

"Not at all. It's nine years, Mateo. That's nothing. Certainly not enough to keep me away from you."

"I'm glad to hear it. Because I do believe you are right, someday you'll be my wife."

"All in God's timing."

He smiled. "Yes, in God's timing."

Nina put all her faith, all of her trust, in that. The Lord had watched over her, brought Mateo to her, and gifted her with the love of her life. She would continue to trust in His perfect will.

EPILOGUE

Nina had grown up going to Mulberry Creek State Park. It was one of her favorite places. She was not about to let anyone, not let any experience, keep her from going there. In fact, she and Mateo had visited the park several times over the past year.

With Conrad Greene behind bars for the rest of his life, she had nothing to fear. He had been convicted of the murders of both Gloria Hanson and Chester Crenshaw. Though his past had been thoroughly investigated, no other suspicious deaths had come to light, while his thievery had proved to be ongoing for nearly a decade.

The items in the lockbox had been returned to their owners, including those that had been discovered after Conrad's arrest.

While her pictures would never hang on the wall of an art gallery, she found that she really did love photography. She'd gotten much better over the past year. Mateo often accompanied her, taking responsibility for Coco and her leash so Nina's hands were free for photos.

She wasn't taking photos today, though. Today they were there for a picnic. It had become one of their favorite weekend pastimes. They both had stressful yet rewarding jobs.

Finding balance was crucial and their picnics had become the perfect way to offset what had often been a trying week.

Mateo had resigned from the Mulberry Creek PD because he'd been looking for a fresh start. He'd gone to work with Cassie, where he found it satisfying to choose his own cases, set his own hours. To date, he'd located a runaway teen, tracked down a small-scale jewel thief, and had helped Cassie with the footwork involved in reuniting several adoptees with the biological families they'd been searching for. Not to mention dozens of smaller cases that still provided him with a sense of accomplishment.

Nina held Coco's leash while Mateo carried the picnic basket. They reached their favorite spot by the river. It was a beautiful, glorious spring day. Nina had heard that the new eaglets had hatched last week. Maybe later they'd wander that way to take a peek.

Mateo set the basket down then flipped the lid open. He pulled out the lightweight blanket that rested on top. He spread it and they had a place to sit.

Coco plunked down on the edge of the blanket. She had bonded with Mateo over the past year, too. He'd finally admitted to Nina that he thought there really was something to those special puppy powers of hers. He'd opened up to Nina about his boys, often while Coco was nestled halfway on his lap. Nina's heart had nearly broken listening to Mateo share the deepest depths of his grief. But now was the time to heal, to start anew, while never forgetting the love he'd had for his sons.

"Can you believe it's been over a year since the day Conrad chased us through the park?" Nina asked.

Mateo arched an eyebrow at her. "Hush now. We don't want to ruin today with thoughts of that man."

"Oh, I know." Nina took a seat on the blanket. "Yet, if

not for him, if not for that day, you and I wouldn't be together right now. God truly does work all things together for good."

"That he does." Mateo sat beside Nina and, for just a moment, they enjoyed the gentle sound of the creek burbling and the leaves rustling. "This year has been one of the best of my life. You helped me turn from being a jaded detective to a man who looks forward to each and every day. You helped me to rediscover my faith. Because of you, I've been able to talk about my boys again, to remember them without feeling as if my heart is being torn from my chest."

Nina reached over and took his hand.

"I love you, Nina. I'm so blessed to have you—and Coco—in my life."

Nina's heart felt full to bursting. "I'm pretty sure I fell in love with you the moment you offered my starving dog your granola bar. I *liked* you before then. Admired you. Thought you were awfully nice to look at." She winked. "But when you gave Coco the only food you had…" She pressed her hand to her heart. "You won me over."

"With a granola bar."

"Yes."

He chuckled.

"It's more than that," she continued. "I love that you want to help others." Mateo had joined her church and, together, they spearheaded the TLC Program, a group of volunteers who helped members of their community with projects like lawn mowing, grocery shopping, and small repairs. Parents were encouraged to volunteer with their children, and Mateo's passion for this gave Nina a glimpse of the sort of father he'd been. Of the sort of father he would, hopefully, be again in the future. "Your kindness and compassion inspire me every day."

She loved this man so much she could hardly bear it.

"Will you marry me?" Nina blurted. "Because I simply don't think I can live without you. I don't want to live without you."

His eyes widened and he stared at her in surprise.

She was suddenly reminded of that long-ago day when Jimmy had held up his hand for a high-five and Mateo had nearly left him hanging. Only now she was the one left hanging, and her heart dipped as silence filled the air.

Then he chuckled.

Her brow furrowed. "That wasn't exactly the response I was hoping for."

Mateo's eyes sparkled and oh, how she loved to see him smile.

"Your exuberance is one of the things that drew me to you," he said. "Even if you are stealing my thunder, so to speak."

"Stealing your—"

She was unable to finish that thought because Mateo had reached into the picnic basket. Instead of pulling out a sandwich, as she was half expecting, he pulled out a small black-velvet box.

Her heart leapt and she bit her lip. It took a moment for her to tear her eyes from the box and look into Mateo's deep brown eyes again.

"Nina," he said, his tone a contradictory mix of seriousness and amusement, "I had this romantic day planned explicitly for the sake of asking you to be my wife." He opened the box and a breathtaking princess-cut solitaire rested inside. "Will you marry me?"

"Yes!" Tears of joy filled her eyes and she threw her arms around Mateo. "Nothing would make me happier."

Coco yipped her agreement, sensing their excitement and

not caring what it was about, as long as her humans were happy.

He squeezed her and Nina melted into his arms, thanking the Lord that Mateo had come into her life.

"Want to try out the ring?" He whispered the words into her ear.

She laughed and pulled away from him. Mateo took the ring from the box and carefully slid it onto her finger. It was a perfect fit, thanks to some guidance from her sister-in-law Cassie, his work partner, who was the only person who knew what he'd planned for the day.

"It's beautiful," she said. "And I think our life together will be beautiful as well."

"How soon are we going to start this life together?"

Nina's hand grazed Coco's back. "We don't have to rush. If you think it would be better to take our time."

"I'm not getting any younger, you know."

She laughed over what had now become a private joke between them. "Then why wait?"

"I see no reason," Mateo said, "no reason at all. I cannot wait to stand before God, our families and our friends, and make you my wife."

He leaned over and kissed her then, a silent promise of their future.

* * * * *

Dear Reader,

Nina and Mateo's book is the last in the Big Sky Series. I've really loved writing this cast of characters featuring the Montgomery family. The siblings are all dealing with the loss of their sister Ella. Each in their own way.

Nina has embraced her faith, drawing closer to God after losing the sister she loved so much. She became a hospice nurse to honor Ella's memory. In our daily lives, we can see so many ways God works things together for good, for those who are called according to His purpose. Nina is an inspiration to Mateo, who lost his family. He sees how she leans into God for comfort, peace, and the promise of Heaven and seeing our loved ones again. Her faith awakens his own dormant faith.

Best wishes,
Amity